TRUE
ENLIGHTENMENT

TRUE
ENLIGHTENMENT

2 BOOKS IN 1

LEE MADDAFORD

authorHOUSE®

AuthorHouse™ UK Ltd.
1663 Liberty Drive
Bloomington, IN 47403 USA
www.authorhouse.co.uk
Phone: 0800.197.4150

Published by AuthorHouse 03/06/2014

ISBN: 978-1-4918-8387-7 (sc)
ISBN: 978-1-4918-8364-8 (hc)
ISBN: 978-1-4918-8401-0 (e)

BOOK 1
TRUE ENLIGHTENMENT

"Religion and Racism, It is very hard to distinguish the two when they are looked at closely with a concerned eye. Fear of a 'higher' being, is matched only by fear of what is unknown. And as for people being tolerant of one another . . . well, wouldn't that make for a peaceful world?"

"Bible bashing preacher!" was the remark that shot through the arena with condemning inaccuracy. "you wish to proclaim world peace, then do your part by keeping your mouth shut!"

Authority had spoken and silent stirrings had once again filled the oval council chamber. Blank and expressionless faces seated like manikin dolls soon shrouded the man into a mist of obscurity and the senate meeting was hastily brought to a close.

"Your wish to preach peace in such dire times is a joke, not only to my ears, but also to the rest of all who hear such lunacy. My child, you will be doing yourself a great favour if you learn to keep such thoughts to yourself!"

Keeping true to form, lifeless rain fell solemnly beneath a darkening sky onto the bustling streets of central London. Clothes of silk sponge soaked in the atmosphere with ease, and the flow of human traffic, swam by like goldfish in a bowl. Standing solitary with everyone beneath a cloud of world depression, it was clear to sense that the day had taken a turn for the worst.

"Hey . . . Hey Gabe, over here!"

The muffled cockney accent was drowned by the noise of traffic, but the determined and forceful manner in which the voice was carried however, quickly shook me from my spiralling apathy and back to my senses.

The man's fluidity looked almost like a lost art as he darted skilfully through the opposing fast lane, and drew ever closer. Coming into clear sight, the man reigned breathlessly to a halt. After a few seconds of recovery, the man stood to his usual enigmatic, and on this occasion, soaking composure.

"See that you made it out alive then" Came the mans upbeat and fluent bass. "raising a taboo subject in these dark days inst always such a good idea, you know. Im surprised you havn't at least been outlawed form the country!"

Taking a reluctant glance at the imposing and ominous marble structure that loomed over my shoulder, I shifted on the spot. Realising that even whilst standing shoulder to shoulder with a brother there was no other body to whom to turn. The senate arena . . . Even on home turf—*eyes to the floor* . . .—My heart sank.

"Im surprised to see you walking the streets" I wistfully greeted . . . "**Sedition** these days is a *crime* that rarely goes unnoticed by those with intent . . ."

Thinking of all those on either side of the Political Fence, and all those in between, Simon welcomed the change of direction, compared to that of the usual up and down. Casting the eye of his mind over a few idiotic and unsavoury scenarios that related to the topic, Simon harrumphed and seemed almost disgruntled in his manner as he spoke,

"If an offset of telling the **undisputed truth** has a tendency to liberate people; mentally, physically, spiritually and whole heartedly—then surely it is plain to se that the true crime, rests on another's conscience . . ."

With the fourth point being made by an outstretched finger, I looked to the thumb and realised they had a point of their own to make . . . Opposable thumbs-up . . . opposition to the constant enmity *riddled* and conceited *confliction* that is the norm of everyday 'life' . . .

. . . Calm, confident and with unfaltering composure, Psi clasped his hands together and looked as though he were about to launch into another of his legendary speeches on the limitless possibilities of the human race. Before he had a chance to deconstruct the entire world around him, however, I decided to cut in,

"I take it you heard the news of today then?"

Creating a disturbance within the automaton flow of traffic, Simon gave a smile and raised his soaking brow,

"In the canteen at lunch, it was all on live-comm. I thought I would change the channel, disturb the usual mind numbing t.v. dum with haste, and enliven everyone with an ear, as to who is responsible for manufacturing and fabricating the world around us! Believe it or not, today's events have actually inspired me! I have visions of next weeks lesson plan coming to fruition . . ."

With my attention momentarily wrangled from the leering marble monstrosity, I briefly pondered how there was any possibility of there being any *positive* avail from such an overbearing travesty. Acknowledging Simon with serious eye and slack jaw surprise, he paid my scepticism in kind, and a response was given as if by reading my mind . . .

"It is said that *all* clouds have a silver lining, my pessimistic brother. But of course, to achieve any kind of positive avail, a scenario may have to be looked at from many angles before any chance of optimism is achieved . . .

"However, on a lighter note, youre sure trying to put the burdening *weight* of 'issues' on the mind of the machine! Beginning to tread on the icy path that is wrought with unstable invisible conspiratorial enemies with ulterior motives, adversary . . ." Psi cut short as he pondered his next glimpse to enlightenment; and opportunists of the 'highest' calibre to the highest bidder . . .

"Beginning to tread . . . we haven't even hit the tip of the ice berg of this desert tundra yet!" Then wistfully to myself "Is there any *real* way to take control . . . ?"

Unrelenting and never ceasing, the mind of a freethinker weighed heavy with unresolved issues. Thinking back to the rabble and tedium of the past 30 minutes instilled nothing but despair. The embers of my angry solitude burned . . .

Simon cracked at my absent-minded trail.

"Ha ha you mean turn all fanatical with candidates who hold blind faith and fearlessness close to their hearts?"

Simon had the excitement of a child as he bounced on the spot.

"Not so much blind, but something like that . . . I take it your in then?"

Simon scoffed,

"You know I was in from the start brother. This needs to be talked about squire, and I know just the place to do it. A proposition one might say.

"Gabriel . . . This is going to be one weekend that you will never forget . . ."

ALCOHOL IS A DRUG.

"So you up for it then?" came Simons—as ever—inquisitive, enthusiastic and persuasive voice. "What do you reckon then, get this Friday night started with a pub crawl?"

The quieter streets of London gave you room to breathe and time to think away from the hustle. The rain still fell, but the thought of sinking a few pints came welcomingly into my forefront of thinking.

"Well Soho this time of night can be kind of rough, but it depends on whether you want to take the country path, or the more scenic route?"

Psi gave a quirky smile as the red lights began to glow ever brighter . . .

"Look at that arse!"

Pretending not to hear, the barmaid went about her business.

"Nice and subtle Psi, just the way I like it . . . Beautiful."

A smile came to my face as the barmaid threw me some bait in the form of a seductive glance.

Grabbing her attention worked. As she walked closer, there was an aura of beauty about her. This woman was gorgeous.

"What can I get you 2 gentlemen this evening?"

Even her voice carried with it the subtle hint of interest and engagement.

"A spit roast!"

This comment brought a giggle, but the cold look which ensued over the bar, soon chilled the mood.

"All we have on the menu tonight boys, is toad in your bum hole . . ."

I hadn't laughed so hard for a long time. Bright red and with his tail between his legs, Psi coughed up enough money for a couple of pints.

Chuckling to a table in a quiet corner of the bar, and leaving the bar maid one—nil up, I thought I would let Psi stew in his juices for a minute.

"Got more than you were bargaining for there!"

Psi gave this comment a thought, and chuckled to himself into his pint glass. Placing the dark ale neatly back onto the beer mat, he sat for a moment in calculating thought.

"How much do you wager I could woo this chick?"

From the tone of voice and the look in his eyes, I could tell he was serious.

"yeah right man." You'd be lucky to get any form of contact other than 'that's £4.80!'"

Simon took another mouthful of beer.

I guarantee you I could get her number. Call it quits at a phone number? Loser buys the next 2 rounds?"

Well Im not stopping you, and I suppose there's nothing to lose . . . except your self-confidence and pride! She's gonna eat you alive!"

Simon was never a man to turn down a challenge, even one that he had concocted entirely on his own. Halfway to the bar, he glanced back with confidence, and the charm was already beginning to show.

Jade had an unspoken mystique about her that was wholly understood, by few—Even by those who 'knew' her. Living through years of mental abuse and tragedy, left her with some 'crazy' ideas about life. One of the more unfathomable—especially to the 'common' people—was the idea that life was just an act, and we were all performing our own individual part, as a character. Coming to terms with her own state of mind, Jade soon became very adept. Sincerity and soulful being was her true art form, and only a fool would ever suspect of otherwise. Charlatanism was the scene that she never wanted to live. Besides, the show already had an all herd cast—of the proverbial sheep, that is ☺.

With deliberate intention in mind, Simon drew up to the bar looking directly at the barmaids chest. The short distance between his seat and empty bar gave him 'ample' time to undress her. Finally arriving at the bar, he rolled his tongue back in and cleared his throat.

"Another couple of pints 'would go down', a treat!"

Sensing the subtle tone of his asking, the barmaid unintentionally broke a slight smile. Diverting attention however, she quickly spun on her heel, and reached to a couple of glasses on the sill.

Going from chest to arse within the space of 10 seconds, left Psi with a smug grin on his face, and he made no effort to change tactics even when she returned to face him. With glasses in hand, the barmaid swooshed casually into pint pouring stance.

Jade was the kind of person who was always willing to give people a second chance. And along with realising that the customers eyes were still focused firmly on her chest, led her to diverting his attention by sparking up a conversation.

With intention to offend,

"So stranger, whats your take on life then? Only wondering, because it seems to me that trying to comprehend people, is not one of your strong points . . ."

Being awoken back to his senses, Simon coolly looked deeply into the barmaids eyes. Feeling a slight connection, he shone a relaxed and easy smile, and decided to start playing properly.

"Hmm . . . Take on life? I could talk to the early hours with a question like that . . . ! Well, I'm a lecturer to a group of very Open Minded Individuals at Keystone College, if you want me to be truthfully honest?!. So as always, today has been another insightful and Enlightening day, as to what Life, is all about!"

With a kindled interest suddenly brewing, the barmaid threw back a glance of attention, and placed the first pint in front of Psi. But unwilling to fold straight away, she continued in a striking manner.

"I was thinking more along the lines of professional lager lout! Or maybe a lecturer to teenagers on how to drink vast quantities of alcohol, and who teaches a GCSE on how <u>not</u> to get your stomach pumped!"

Psi was taken aback. The display of deadly venom being spewed forth from this beautiful woman was a nightmare scene for him, and one that he had not quite come to expect.

"Sharp Darlin. Well you got it half right, we save that part of the curriculum for the sponsored nights out! But most of the time we are busy discussing topics on what would change the world for the better!"

Judging from the sincerity in Simons voice, Jade decided to relent a little, and continued in a mutually respecting manner.

"Keystone college you say? I used to be a student there myself about 4 years ago! I was looking for dome deeper meaning to life, and decided to pursue a degree in Psychology. 4 Years of studying certainly gave me an insight into a boring outlook on life, but I have always felt that something wasn't quite right. As if something has always been missing . . ."

Turning her attention from Simon, and looking vacantly into a half filling pint glass, Jade stood for a moment in reflection. Sensing the sudden stop in momentum, Psi brought the mood up a little.

"Hey sister!, why did you stop going to college? The course that I lecture now, would teach you soo much, that you would never have even thought about before! This would probably be the link that has been missing from your Consciousness!. Have you ever heard about True Enlightenment? It is like a Philosophy of the Mind, but instead of just speculating to find more questions, you speculate to find proper answers!"

Elegantly placing the second pint onto the mahogany bar, Jade looked affectionately into Simons as ever, welcoming eyes.

"That's £4.80 Please."

Simon thoughtfully placed the money into her outstretched hand.

"I have heard a bit about Enlightenment, it seems to be quite a recognised concept these days. With hushed talks of the start pf a 'Revolution', along with finding true inner Peace and the like. But I have never really endeavoured to find out what it truly means. Don't get me wrong, Psychology did open my eyes in the sense of how closed minded some people can be, but something in the world still doesn't feel quite right to me. I feel as though there is a part of my life that is missing. I guess you could say that it makes me feel kinda Numb."

A thoughtful silence fell upon the bar. Briefly pondering over the cash register and stirring innocently on the spot, Jade fished out 20 pence change. Shaking the coins in her hand on the return to face Simon, she playfully outstretched her hand. Receiving the change with similar acknowledgement, Psi placed the coins into his jean pocket.

"I used to feel exactly the same darlin, and it is truly refreshing to hear an Individual such as yourself, endeavouring to think Outside of the Box! You just need to find the proverbial Light with inside yourself, and I guarantee that you will feel whole again. It sounds to me like you need some form of guidance at the moment though. Spiritual guidance darlin, you should seriously consider trying to understand what this Truly means! Help yourself to be Truly Free! I urge you to jump on board the Enlightenment boat and to try and Enlighten all other people out there, who are weighed down and are naively drowning in this sea of unConciousness!"

Feeling a slight warmth emanating from the bar, I looked over at the rosy cheeks of a blushing Beauty. In the space of 5 minutes, I watched Simon work his wonder, as the woman stood in admiration of his sentiment and honesty.

Watching the barmaid rummage under the bar to produce a notebook, I knew only too well that the deed had already been done. No sooner had Simon put the folded paper in is jacket pocket, was he triumphantly returning to the table with a big grin on his face . . .

Striking hard, I surveyed the table with a keen eye. The break was a favourable one. Potting a yellow, and with the ball set up nicely for the next shot, I relaxed, and continued with confidence.

Lining up for the next shot, I could sense the delight that was hovering at the other end of the table.

Looking up from the table,

"I must admit man, you handled yourself pretty well!. I never knew you had it in you. I'm impressed!"

Striking with precision, another yellow rolled perfectly between the rims of the pocket. I stalked calculatingly to my next shot.

"Looks like you have been practicing . . . I never remember you being this good. Your gonna kick my arse at this rate!"

Standing tall and confidently, just a foot beneath the dark oak beams of the pub, Simon drank a good half pint in the space of a few seconds, as the prospect of his losing the game began to sink in.

Chuckling to myself, I lined up to take the next shot.

"I'm gonna try not to even give you a chance . . . I know your like a fuckin wizard when it comes to pool!"

Simon's reply was a humorous close eyed and smiling, nod of agreement.

"So whats her name then? You were talking for ages! I drifted off after a while, but what I heard definitely gave me the impression that the place would soon be ablaze, from the amount of sparks that were flying through the air!"

Following through, Simon opened his eyes, and shone a knowing stare. Meeting his look half way, a couple of seconds passed, and the dramatic effect was allowed to sink in.

"I told you man. You just need to have a little bit more faith in the intricate worings of the master . . ."

Simon broke off, and took a large swig of beer. Picking up on the humour in his voice, I decided to play along.

"Intricate workings indeed . . . Is that what you told your shrink last night?"

Simon casually took a sip of beer. Following suit, I walked casually to my next shot.

"Isnt that the fourth one now? Heard on the grapevine that psychiatrist suicides have tripled in the past 3 days like . . ."

Smiling to the tip of my cue, I could sense the mechanics of Simons humour igniting.

"Yeah well that's nothing compared to what I heard yesterday on the olive branch, I heard that you were the man they all sought help from!"

Simons sharp wit never ceased to cause gratuitous amounts of laughter. Accepting 'defeat' and hanging my head in shame from 'losing' the battle of droll, I added insult to injury, and proceeded to miss the next shot. Damn.

Time to take a few more sips of beer . . .

Achieving his rightful position, Simon soon let the 'table' know who was boss. The first ball was bludgeoned to 90% death, and was more than happy to cower in its new hole-like dwelling. As usual, another perfect shot from the Buddha of the pooling world.

The balls on the table trembled helplessly as their own impending doom loomed over them like a Zeusonian strom cloud.

"That's how you play man, make the balls cower . . ."

Simon was never too afraid to throw an innuendo into any situation, and mounting the table was another prospect we all had to look forward to. Maybe.

Thundering over to the other side of the table, Simon stole his victim, and was ready to cast judgement with his pugilistic pole of punishment. Blasted to 95% intensity this time round, the ball only just managed to stay in one piece. After meeting its maker, the Quaker was swallowed hungrily by the sink-hole at the far end of the table. Simon gave a smug grin of execution, and in his state of furious and judgemental wrath, all he could see was red . . .

Being defeated twice within the space of 10 minutes, did not bode well for the preconception of a taunt free and placid evening. Time to resolve the situation beofre it had a chance to get out of hand . . .

"Look how smug those last 3 yellows are man, I think that they're prayers must have paid off . . . Close game brother!"

Holding his weapon in a self satisfied and accomplished stance, Simon smiled and looked at me in a—not so bad after all then squire—kind of manner . . . Appreciating the sincerity in my voice, Simon continued in a respecting, but none the less triumphant manner.

"Just as well I let you go first . . . Otherwise there really would have been something to rib you about!"

Accepting defeat gracefully, I placed my cue neatly back on the rack. Turning to my pint, I decided to drown my sorrows and drained the last quarter. Simon looked intently at his dry glass, and silently ushered me toward the bar.

"Guess the next 2 rounds are on you buddy . . . Her name is Jade."

Discretion was another form which Simon had chosen to master, and I knew only too well, when he chose to put it into further practice.

"Nice and subtle Psi . . . Ill be back in 5 minutes."

"No worries dude, have fun . . . ! I shall keep myself amused with the jukebox, definitely Time for a bit of the Dark Side . . . Reckon that its time to Break the Wall—united we stand, rather than divided . . ."

Half way to the bar, the sentiment rang through, and the chimes of a very familiar song immediately began to toll. Jestered to the bar—to the sound of my favourite tune—it was clear to sense, that the king of subtlety, had officially been crowned.

On this occasion, I was more than happy to have lost the bet. With windows that shone so openly, it was impossible not to notice the sudden warmth that ran through both of our beings. This woman was truly beautiful.

Aquarius—Libra: Pupils Deeply dilating, on the evenly balanced scales of True Understanding. Love.

Encumbering to the bar in the form of a lumbering beast, I skilfully juggled the empty glasses into an underarm forte, which allowed me to fish my moth free wallet from my pocket. A couple of seconds from the bar, I flashed a cheeky grin. A calm, cool and clear water was free to flow, after the melting of the ice.

With seductive motion, combined with the welcoming and ardent smile of a goddess—made my heart miss a beat . . . Gazing with earnest into the most open and shining eyes I had ever seen, was all that was needed for the mutual Self Realisation, that true Love, actually existed . . . I never felt this way until this moment, and I Know, that the feeling was More than mutual . . .

. . . At the bar—

Leaning fixedly with a wrench-like grip on the protruding shaft labelled 'wife beater', was a working art form, that made me chuckle.

"How are you going to top that then stranger . . . ? Your friend is a very clever man . . ."

With no immediate answer, I dexterously placed the glasses on the bar. And before I could answer . . .

"So, Same—again stranger . . . ?"

A couple of seconds passed, and with a look of contemplation, I engaged the playful subtlety of her asking . . .

"Fundamentally, but different—all the same . . . Another couple Would, go down a treat."

With a flirtatious smile, her hand effortlessly slid down as the pressure on the tap was slowly released. If the tap wasn't rock solid before, it was now. At this stage, we were both way beyond chemistry. This was Physicality, and there was definitely an exothermic response rising from the groin area.

"Soo . . . you want clever then . . . ? Well . . . uh, will common sense do.? It seems to prevail in most situations . . ."

A second of thought was allowed to pass,

"Well—in concurrence to the song, the dull day has ticked away, and I hope that you chose to use your Time constructively, rather than frittering and wasting your hours in some off hand way . . . ?"

Apprehending the sentiment, a reverent quiet fell over the bar. The first pint had been poured and suddenly my attention was diverted to the return of a tightening chokehold around the tap . . . The flirtatious smile slowly returned, and the frothing head of the second pint, slightly spilled over the rim.

Delicately placed next to its beer-like counterpart, they looked onward at theyre dogged fodder-ridden brethren and got an accurate picture of the fate that awaited them.

Glancing at one another with a look of paralysed desperation, they were seconds away from realising that their only salvation, was the cleansing and sobering experience that awaited them at the end of they're short life. I looked hungrily at one of the pints . . . "Ahhhhh . . ."—

"That was refreshing . . . !"

—Placing the beer next to the pint . . .

"Dude . . . wheres your head!" . . .

. . .

A religious-free baptism had just taken place at the far end of he bar, and the cleansed glasses gleamed stoically as they were Care-Fully placed back next to their stoic brothers.

PLaying a £5 note flatly on the bar with both hands, was the only way that I could fathom—successfully luring the attention of this serene siren, as she purposely busied herself with other bar-like paraphernalia. I waited with baited breath . . . but her alluring peripherals, were reeling Me in. Time to try another spot . . .

Deciding to discard the rod, I couldn't help myself but to wade further into deeper water . . . Right, arms folded, elbow on the bar . . . Rook(ie) to Queen . . . The Castle Keeps you in check-mate . . .

Making progress, I was sinking . . . time to fill this Led Balloon Scenario with more hot air . . .

"Clever he may be, but that's not the real reason behind why no man could ever 'compete' with a man of Simons stature . . ."

Halt-! The paraphernalia stood to attention, as a sudden look of interest was directed toward the juke box . . .

With seriousness . . .

"I mean look at that hair!"

With the flowing, golden and luscious locks of a beanpole as the centre point of attention, I was able to pounce.

With a slight chuckle,

"Most women are jealous, and your one of the first that hasn't turned green . . . Good on you . . . ! You control your rage well."

The defences had been breached, and I was pretty sure that the garrisoned 'hostiles' would soon relent . . .

Meeting my smug half way, with a comical significance,

"That's because red isnt my colour, Im more of an ambient yellow kind of girl . . ."

The sign was clear that at this crucial stage, it was either stop.—or a free pass to mile upon mile of open high way.

"And you truly shine . . . !"

Shyness suddenly fell on the other side of the bar, and the paraphernalia resumed its tedium. There was me thinking that red wasn't her colour. It wasn't. I quickly changed the subject . . .

"On a lighter note however, you still havnt answered my question . . . You know the one pretty much along the lines of 'have you had a good day?'"

The clutter was quickly organised neatly back into its usual position, and was soon out of mind. With an unexpected sigh . . . ,

"Well coming into work always seems to have a way of prolonging an already tedious day. But apart from that, It seems that things seem to be livening up a bit . . . !"

. . . I was taken aback as a playfully amorous smile shone warmly from the confines of the bar. The strings of my heart played in harmony to this breathtaking melody, but such a moment can only last for so long

. . . At that moment, a cold air of discord thundered into the bar. The oak door was slammed shut by the howling wind, and the cause of the vacuum, appeared to be devoid of any logic . . . the Bum note of Neolithic 'wisdom' that trembled through the air, ambled to the bar, and shuddered as he continued in a broken manner. Already, this man was getting on my nerves . . .

Groggily clearing his throat, the man removed his sodden jacket and took a seat.

Cheerily intercepting her new customer—

"A pint and a large whisky . . ."

. . . His lack of manners struck more dis-chord and before the scenario turned into a parody, I apprehended them from the far end of the bar with a look of—'they don't cost a thing'. Part of the acknowledgement was making sure that he was the first to look away, and after this acquiescence was adhered to, I redirected my look with confidence and reassurance . . .

The stranglehold around the wife-beater returned . . .

Meeting his look for a second time, I thought that I would break the ice.

In a respecting tone,

"Hows it goin this evening man? Are you well . . . ?"

A look of what appeared to be borderline disgust, was the only reply that was thrown in my direction. Calmly catching it, I threw it back in his face with a confident smile of, 'if your going to be cheeky, I will tear you a new hole . . . '

. . . His look soon folded once again, and with a mutual respect, his pint thumped the bar as it was placed in front of him with disregard.

A stand still fell upon the bar, as the first song ended . . .

Accompanied by the opening riff to 'Communication-Breakdown', Simon coolly made his way to the bar. The three of us shared a comical greeting of respectful smiles . . . A large whisky thumped at the end of the bar . . .

. . . It was smiles' all Round . . . Cheers!

The 3rd round had just been rinsed, and the uninterrupted cheer remained. The gentleman's spectator 5th finished the bottle, and a slight feeling of hostility was beginning to brew, as the alcoholic state osmotised through to mainstream . . .

. . . The enlightening topic of financial gain versus Equality not only had us all enthralled; it also seemed to have the subtle ability of being a malevolent attention grabber . . . The topic soon branched into race equality versus world peace, and the drunken mannerisms at the end of the bar, soon began to stir . . .

"So your basically saying that there are *Reasons* as to why World Peace hasn't been created yet.!?"

Jade served as the constant refreshment, that most men crave and desire . . . Simon was the man doing the talking, but I was the man with the looks . . .

Simon chuckled as his head dropped toward the bar with a look of slight disdain,

"Huh . . . Why world peace hasn't been created yet . . . Where to get started on that one . . . !"

Knowing the real reasons why this was the case, always seemed like bit of a paradox to Simon.

He was always willing to Fight for Peace, and this small conversational *battle*, was to help eliminate the battalion of Naivety . . .

"Well . . . since the day we were born—corrupt, spoon fed—Misinforma—" . . .

Simon was cut short as an empty glass was slammed at the far end of the bar . . .

. . . Momentarily distracted, Simon took a brief glimpse over his left shoulder, and with unfaltering composure, returned to face both of us whilst continuing to comically jive with the rhythm of the music. With cold shoulder, toned voice and intention in mind, he fanned the flames of kindling deadwood . . . a legendary speech was to be his tool . . .

. . ."One example as to why this is the case, is if you look at how schools were operated around 50 years ago . . . Deliberately Indoctrinated by a school system that taught prejudice and Fear. This system basically **told** them, that this is the correct way to *live*. I mean no wonder that a Lot of people from that era still walk around with their eyes closed, and *suffer* a life crippled by reciprocated enmity . . . ! They have yet to grow up . . ."

Taking a mouthful of beer, me and Simon gave a mutual cheers. Simon asked an open-ended rhetorical question . . .

"Wouldn't you agree with that . . . ?"

The three if us smiled at one another as the hostility emanating from the end of the bar intensified and began to glow . . .

Simons soul purpose of that moment was to burn up every kind of fuel that came in his general direction. Feeling the heat, Simon thoughtfully placed his glass onto the bar, and continued in a relentless manner . . .

"In other words, these people have no clue as to what they are Angry at. They don't even realise they are angry and there are reasons as to why this is the case—so they lash out at anyOne, or anything that doesn't conform to their unloving standard of hate. Suffice to say, a lot of them are so frustrated by their lack of Understanding, that they point a condemning and judgemental finger at everything, but the real issue that hangs around everyones neck. They would rather stop other people enjoying their own time in Peace, in place of apprehending a way to make their own life better. They would rather lead a blind life consumed by Naïve ignorance, rather than facing the true issue that is ruining their Own life, as well as others—and therefore each others . . .

"Ultimately they are Cowards . . ."

Simon took another mouthful of beer and had an air of confidence about him that was bordering on being cocky. Smiling to himself in a self-satisfied manner, he asked the same open-ended question . . .

This time however, a reply was given . . .

Rising from the throat in the form of a semi-drunken slur . . .

"You little bastard . . . You don't know the first thing about life"

Manifesting itself physically, the chair that seated the suffering torment, slammed into the wall as it flew half way across the room . . .

Lumbering towards his left in an energetic frenzy was soon to be the drunkards sobering experience and enlightening mistake. Simon did not move until the last second . . .

Jerking his elbow just shy of the drunkards nose, gave Simon a second of stunned time to wrap his arm around the mans neck. With a sharp and sudden jerk of the hips, the man was thrown away and landed in a heap a few feet from the bar . . .

In a state of drunken rage, the man quickly came around for a second bought and charged. A fist, swung again from the hips, connected squarely to his dinted chin and knocked him to the floor once more . . . Simon quickly stood over him . . .

"You had better calm down old man, before you get hurt . . ."

Controlled breathing, kept the situation calm . . .

Dragging the drunken state to the tabled partition opposite the bar, Simon grabbed the mans stubbled and aged jaw, and looked him squarely in the eye . . .

"Have you not learned how to have a discussion yet grand-pa . . . ? You now the ones along the lines of knowing when to Listen—and then having something constructive to say—after you have given the notion a moment of Thought.!?"

Continuing in a forceful manner,

"Its our generation that are opening your feckless eyes you belligerent fool, and you cant stand it . . . Get a life you drunkard . . . something Other than the one that revolves around yourself and *Trying* to ruin others'" . . .

The song ended, and the bar was still once again. The wind howled outside . . .

A few minutes passed and Simon jostled the frail gentleman, onto one of the seats at the partition just next to the juke-box.

A pint of water was soon placed attentively on the table, as the man conscientiously drank. His shaking frailty soon began to cease, as his wake was accompanied by the opening aura of 'coming back to life . . .'

"Knowing when to listen brother . . . It is one of the biggest parts of life. If you teach yourself to listen hard enough, you may then one day, learn how to Love . . ."

Simon left the man to his own devices as he walked selflessly back to the bar, picking his pint, he took a mouthful. The earlier cheer returned—uninterrupted . . .

"How on earth are we gonna chase that one up . . . ?"

Even before there was a second of thought, Jade already had the shot glasses in hand . . .

The salt and lime of the tequila slammer certainly seemed to hit the spot. I was now finding it hard to keep my eyes form her, as she flirtatiously and elegantly laboured behind the bar. Simon cleared his throat . . .

"So continuing on before we were rudely interrupted, what are your thoughts concerning race and equality . . . ?"

After suffering the effects of tequila stammering, the gentleman's ears pricked . . .

"Well . . . seeing as you're the man who knows everything there is to know, why don't you enlighten us . . ."

The man's pricked ears were replaced, with a placing of his almost empty pint glass . . .

"South Africa, this is probably the best place to start . . . I take it you have been watching the news recently?"

My time as senator was primarily preoccupied with study, writing and free-styling on the guitar. The TV never really held much interest with me . . .

"You know I don't buy the papers these days . . . Second hand news about how fucked up the world is and what not . . ."

"Exactly . . . How fucked up the world is."

Simon piped up,

"You listening Grand-pa . . . ?"

There was no reply.

"Now, Zimbabwe is just like a pawn in this world wide game of chess, but what is going on there, is small time news compared to what the rest of the world is up to . . ."

Simon always managed intrigue to a T.

"You see why I say the bit about race Grand-pa, there should be **no** racism any more . . . there are more important issues that need to be dealt with like **Peace**, you moron . . ."

Clearing my throat,

"Come on Psi, I think he's got the message . . ."

"Not yet he hasn't brother, because I haven't finished Talking . . ."

Stalwartly rising from his chair, the rejuvenated man came to the bar for a second pint. Simon slightly nodded to the gentleman, and in a good natured and respecting manner, the now sobering gentleman had a positive aura about him nullified the need for any fretting. A silent respecting was shown all round . . .

"First things first . . . I take it you now who Mugabe is . . . ?"

The man placed the second pint of water to his lips, took a lasting mouthful and placed his drink back onto the bar. With a respecting frankness to his voice . . .

"Yeah . . . he's that Elitist war mongering 80 year old who starves and massacres his own people . . ." the man paused as a grimace filled his face. "Talk of mutilating people if they voted for the democrats over him."

A slight pause of intrigue to the man's knowledge . . .

"Your pretty much spot on there Grand-pa, but that's only half the story. They are only little fishies compared to the white supremacist—Imperialists that really control everything . . . or am I saying too much out loud . . ."

We all shared a slight smug to this serious and enigmatic topic, but there was an air of seriousness to Simons tone. A few seconds passed . . .

"Right, I'll start from scratch . . .—White colonists go to Zimbabwe to cultivate and farm the land for the benefit of the people. Under Mugabe's Rule, everything is fine. Then all of a sudden, Mugabe sees these white settlers as invaders and he orders his followers to destroy and ransack all of the cultivated land! The white settlers are forced by pain of death to leave, and what is left is baron landscape, which the local inhabitants have no idea how too farm . . . They lack education under Mugabes iron fist and all the aid that is sent there is basically spent on keeping a fascist hierarchy in power. Weapons and what not . . . AK47's in the hands of every African child is what their hierarchy wants at the moment. The money is kept by the fascist state rather than empowering the people . . ."

The spiel which reeled so naturally from Simon's tongue, had us all mesmerised as to what was coming next . . .

"Guess who stands there watching the situation get worse. Need I say it . . . ? The Western world and our life of luxury of course. Peace Talks, no action."

Simon was in full flow and there was no slowing him down, "There are reasons why there is no peace in this trigger happy hoedown, will there ever be any justice!?"

After Simons momentary deconstruction to reconstruct, the now sober man took a solitary mouthful of pure water and seated himself at the bar . . . We all joined in unison as we thought of the plight of third world tyranny compared to that of our own life of consuming and miserable luxury . . .

"The logical conclusion is that it could all be resolved tomorrow. But people are soo wrapped up in their own turmoiled little world, that they think of nothing else, other than themselves, twinned with the fact that the banks are hoarding all of the money . . ."

Simons anger began to show . . .

"People have been *kept* blind by the *powers that be* and have been spoon fed siphoned mis-information since day one which has been brought to us via the media. With blind sight we our brothers and sisters as the enemy, and our society is kept in enmity . . . But what can One man do about it other than tell things how they truly are . . . ?"

After all these years of knowing Simon, I never fully appreciated his sentiment toward peace until this evening. I felt butterflies in my stomach from his rousing stimulating truth and wished that I had started paying more attention to the real dealings of the world sooner . . .

"People live in a 3 dimensional world, where a 2 dimensional mentality is the norm. When shown something from a new perspective, they are astounded, and then bemused as to why they didn't see it before. The gullible sheep who still lack the ability of foresight and to see things from more than one angle make up the majority of our populace . . . and they are the ones that 'happily' and naively comply with this invisible imprisonment. They are the ones who Consume, and lead a life of selfish luxury that eats away at the world and 90% of people in it!"

Simon relaxed a little and took a mouthful of beer,

"They are misguided by misinformation, and talking the Undisputed Truth is a physical means of weaning these little lambies from their childish and sheep like behaviour. Some accept this change and decide to grow up, by realising the part they play in this life—whereas the stubborn old fools of the world who refuse to accept this truth, even when there is concrete evidence put before them . . . they are the ones that require a special effort, and weigh everyone else down . . ."

The blustering wind was a bitter, but none the less welcoming—sobering experience. The time was just before 12, and a full golden moon was held gracefully in the starry night sky.

Standing shoulder to shoulder with Psi as we walked through the still busy main streets of London, I thought about the eloquence and beauty that I had just encountered . . . The traffic gave a likeable background and was twinned with the distant banter of human activity.

"What are your plans now then squire . . . ? Got anything that needs immediate and ruthless attention and conviction . . . ?"

I smiled as Simon playfully exaggerated my usually mundane Saturday morning activities.

"Sweet FA man, as always . . ."

Simon quickly cut in—

"Good . . ."

With an air of curiosity to my asking . . .

"How about yourself bro? Got any scenarios planned that require the Simon touch . . . ?"

We shared a mutual chuckle. The laughter was quickly brought round . . .

"Siobhan . . . She's throwing a house party tonight, she says your More than welcome . . ."

Simon gave a nudge and the obligatory wink that accompanied the Bain of a single man as he played out his meddling suggestions.

"Sounds like a plan man, and yes, I know she's married . . . Should we take some wine or something . . . ?"

"No need man, got an eight of pot in my pocket, I'm sure that should be enough for one of her parties . . . You've never been before have you? Telling you now man, your in for a treat."

"Sounds good . . . Lead on Macduff . . ."

I had never before met Siobhan, but Psi often mentioned her in conversation. Every time her name was mentioned however, I always felt negative connotations associated with her. The reason being that each time her name was mentioned, so was her husband's. He was some sort of entrepreneur, and his name was Lucifer . . .

20 minutes of brisk walking had both of our hearts beating healthily. The bitter wind still remained, but felt as though it was beginning to calm. We both felt the inner warmth of our Dutch courage as we once again reached the quieter streets. Out of nowhere, Simon sparked up a joint . . .

Puffing away and holding his breath to maximise the effect, he soon passed me the joint, I took a couple of tokes and continued to walk in a relaxed and contemplative manner . . .

"Nice one bro . . ."

A silence of shared contemplation was the accompaniment with the calming wind . . .

"Isn't she one of the most beautiful women you've ever seen . . . ?"

Arriving at a row of houses, we stopped at the one that had trimmed ivy all the way up to the third story . . . This was a rich part of town, but for some contemplative reason, I couldn't help feeling, that this was the only truly rich house out of the lot.

Rich on all occasions—especially now. The warming vibes that are related with good company, could be felt emanating from the house. Trailing up the shingled pathway, Simon rang the doorbell.

"Looking forward to an awesome evening . . . ?"

Laughter was the accompaniment to the vibrant light that shone with the opening of the door.

"Simon, how are you . . . ? Glad that you have been able to make it!"

Sincerity was the feeling of the moment as Psi casually kissed Siobhan on the cheek.

Recovering from her assault,

"You must be Gabriel.!?"

Expecting a hand-shake I was caught off guard as she lunged from the confines of her home, and gave me a hug!

"I have very much been looking forward to meeting you Gabriel! So cliché, but I have heard soo much about you . . . !"

Caught by surprise again, I looked over at Simon with puzzled bewilderment . . .

Siobhan chuckled . . .

"No need for alarm though . . . we're only concerned with positive news here Gabriel . . ."

After walking into the grandeur entrance and closing the door, the enveloping party atmosphere could instantaneously be felt. The stairwell was occupied by a couple of people excitedly flirting with one another, and the opening to the kitchen on the far right was buzzing with people holding glasses of wine close to their chest. I confidently acknowledged other smartly dressed guests along the way as Siobhan led us to the kitchen . . .

"What can I get you two fine gentlemen this evening . . . ? There are beers in the fridge and a selection of wines in the cooler . . ."

The informal atmosphere was made known. Following through, I caught a couple of smartly dressed eyes that reminded me of those that shone earlier in the evening . . .

Looking to the cooler there was a selection of varying white red and rose wines.

"A glass of your finest White Grenache would go down a treat . . . !"

Siobhan gracefully filled a large wine glass until it was three-quarters full,

"And yourself Gabriel . . . ?"

Feeling a slight pinch from coming empty handed . . .

"A beer would go down a treat . . . Cheers . . . !"

Opening the can and taking a mouthful,

"I take it your drinking this evening . . . ?"

With silent acknowledgement, Siobhan led the two of us with our drinks in hand, through to the main room. Paintings bathed in ambient light were the accompaniment to respectfully chatting guests down the hall, and the real entrance to the home, was made known . . .

"Wow, I have never seen a place like this . . ."

The eight-foot wide arching entrance was unhindered from any angle. The three of us entered into the room.

"Impressive eh . . ."

I found myself lost for words as almost 20 pairs of eyes shone openly in our direction . . . unhindered by any obstructions, my eyes quickly adjusted as I took in the spectacle. Some of the eyes lingered longer than necessary, but I cold tell that it was 90% good company that Siobhan kept Simon's gesture showed that he knew some of the company in the crowd. My eyes were quickly attracted to the gourmet-buffet table at the centre . . .

"Make yourselves at home gentlemen . . . I shall be back before you know it! Don't be afraid to introduce yourselves . . . !"

Siobhan was an excellent host . . . After leaving us for 10 minutes, she was quickly back to see us filling our faces with the most exquisite food that I had eaten in a long time . . .

"I see that you have managed to find some of your college brethren . . . ! Thought that it wouldn't be long before you all started joining in the buffet circuit!"

"Well you know that the College canteen is where I get most of my business these days!"

This half-truth was a perfect ice melting experience . . . a group of about 6 of us were at the centre of the party and the room came to a mutual quiet as the banter livened up. The interest took a respecting hold on the majority of others in the room, but even so, some of the envious eyes still lingered . . .

"So yeah . . . Apparently those that have started to use more than 10% of their brain function are persecuted by the psychiatrist hierarchy and basically downtrodden and banged up for 2 years at a time, no questions asked . . . ! This persecution is mainly focused on those that have found their inner voice that allows them to communicate without moving their lips . . ."

Simon was a man of important knowledge, knowledge that set people free. He always had the perfect knowledge to back up any one of his statements, as he said that it was our younger but mainly older and anger riddled brethren, that are always willing to start an argument. Psi was always the man that resolved them . . .

"I mean, how can people find this justifiable . . . ?"

A dumbfounded quiet filled the room as the statement was digested by the masses. Silence was the only answer. Helping Simon out from his position under the spotlight of many eyes . . .

"I heard that even with the law on his side, they basically locked him up and threw away the key . . ."

Simon placed his food on the table and carried on in an excited manner,

"Exactly . . . Keep him from spreading the peaceful and undisputed truth that telepathy is real. It made me sick when one of my closest friends Neil was locked away. Forced medication against his will and toting around language like ECT and neuro-surgery . . . He is still there . . ."

Psi had the party enthralled.

"Yep . . . he is a peaceful man that hasn't done anything wrong. He has been victimised and psychoanalysed by 'the professionals', and they have basically condemned him for his beliefs. Not only have they taken away his freedom of speech, they have locked him away for 2 years. He is still there! Talk like this holds no hope for a peaceful future . . . It just Shows how inhuman some people can be, and how little we have grown as a race from the persecuting which hunts of the dark ages. He is one of my best friends and he says that the hospital is killing him!"

There was no longer any condemning eyes, as the psycho Analysers of the group began to realise their mistake.

"On a lighter note, I remember him saying that to get people to show their anger and lack of resolve, he would say that he was God and the Devil. This really got on their case, self diagnosis of apparent 'bi polar'. That part gave me a chuckle . . ."

———

Sensing that the social occasion had slowed, Siobhan went around offering refills of drink for everyone. The beer was going down nicely, but a glass of wine after a speech like that . . . ! I headed to the kitchen . . .

Looking at the clock on the wall, it read 1.30 am Saturday morning. The majority of the guests were saying their farewells, but a quiet handful of voices were still around. These are the die-hard guests that stay until the early hours.

Another 30 minutes passed and with renewed vigour, Siobhan and the remaining company sat comfortably around in the living room . . .

Simon rolled a joint, and joyous eyes welcomed the illegal substance into the room . . . Talking . . . this party was just getting started.

"ECT . . . ?"

Simon finished rolling his masterpiece and brought the ashtray close to his side. Simon sparked the joint and took a couple of hefty draws. He blew out 2 big plumes of smoke and replied to the question . . .

"Electro-convulsive therapy"

Placing the joint in the appropriate groove of the ashtray, Simon passed the spell binding propaGanga in my direction . . . Simon continued . . .

"Sounded like he had it pretty heavy in his life too, and even now at his humble age of 20, they seem more than happy to pile more shit onto his plate . . . Trying to electri fry his brain so that he conforms to the social standard of what is classed as normal . . .

The dude who broke the silence piped up . . .

"Well surely if the doctors see this as the appropriate means of treat . . ."

Simon immediately broke in with vehemence . . .

"Stop there—right now . . . Have you not listened to a word that I have said . . . ? So you're going to tell me that this is the price that you have to pay for true individuality . . . ?"

Simon metaphorically took one of his studious acolytes by the scruff of the neck . . .

"Seriously Mark . . . Don't go down this path of closed mindedness with me, you will just annoy me . . ."

Taking my second puff of marijuana, I gave Simon a nod of acknowledgement, and passed the joint to Siobhan . . .

Piping up from the ashes, I decided to break in and support Simon . . .

"Come on bro, keep up . . . ! You should learn to see things from Every angle and not from this closed minded and blind perspective we were just talking about!"

Swallowing a mouthful of potato chips, I looked directly with seriousness at Mark . . .

"You should have seen the fight that broke out in the pub earlier this evening . . . Don't start messing around bro, or you will regret it."

The young man in his early 20s heeded the friendly warning. He happily received the ashtray, and allowed Simon to continue unhindered. With a cheeky smirk . . .

"Yeah . . .—earlier tonight . . . We were peacefully talking about South Africa and people in general, then some belligerent angry old fool thought that it was appropriate to try and attack me . . . ! Out of nowhere . . . ! I could see it coming a mile off, and he soon learned his lesson . . ."

The ash from Mark was tapped into the tray with slight disdain— the tray was passed back to Simon as Mark blew out his 3rd plume of smoke . . .

"Damn right he did, you damn near knocked his head clean off his body—gratifying his anger with your cooling and sobering wrath . . ."

Simon chuckled,

"Cheers bro, that's the best compliment that I have had in a long time! . . ."

Siobhan piped . . .

"Zimbabwe and the like you say . . . ? I know a bit about it . . . Mugabe rigging elections and massacring his people . . ."

Siobhan broke off . . .

"It seems that you have something more to say Siobhan . . . Goodness . . . Do not be afraid to speak! There isn't more of a freedom at your disposal . . . ! But then again . . ."

Another mutual quiet fell over the four of us . . .

Breaking the spell . . .

"Well, there was the time that China sent over arms and Munitions to South Africa to aid Mugabe's regime! Luckily however, the Peaceful Democrats known as the DMC turned these arms and munitions away at Zimbabwe . . ."

Simon smiled . . .

"The right to freedom of speech Siobhan . . . Do you see why some people get locked away no questions asked.!?"

A rhetorical quiet fell over the 4 of us . . . Siobhan continued,

"All of the warmongering autocrat Elite and their mission are made known to few in this world, therefore they are still the ones that remain in power."

Mark yawned and made a spectacle . . .

"Sadly, this seems to make perfect sense to me now you mention. Even in our days of Westernised Luxury, they are still plighted in the third world with Starvation, Aids and Malaria . . . It makes me sick . . ."

Clinking his ringed finger around his wine glass and nodding in reverence, Simon broke in . . .

"Round of applause . . .—that's the kind of talk that gets us somewhere Mark . . . ! Distracting your eye by using the Olympic games as subterfuge for their dark deeds. You cant even wave a flag in public in China without being asked to stop by the police, is that really a world that you want to live in? Even China see fit to lock up and torture those who speak the truth against their regime . . . It seems that wherever you look these days, a populace always suffers in some way shape or form from this global and tyrannical reign of terror. The whole world suffers, for the sake of a handful of *people*, something needs to be done."

Paranoia was something that I was expert at, and I knew when windows to the Soul shone at me . . . this being one of those occasions . . .

"The Senate . . ."

Siobhan kept true to form as an excellent host. The wine that we were drinking was always kept flowing, and Psi was keen to keep the circle alive with his pennies worth. The time was bordering 3am.

"You have never heard of Lucid dreams . . . ? I'm shocked Mark . . . ! Well . . . You're in for a real treat here . . . !"

Talking about family and past history was the topic of the moment. Briefly mentioning that I had met my dead mother in my dreams brought around a studious and empathic sense, and it had stirred something in Simon that I had never seen before. Death and decay was my standing looking to the past, whilst present and future events, showed little signs of improvement.

"Dreaming . . . , but Realisation that you are dreaming. Lots of concentration required here Loved Ones . . . Flying . . . Sex . . . You name it. Anything you want to do, just imagine . . . but of course whilst all the time Obeying the laws of Equality and having self control—as these are the laws of heaven. It is the dream world that we enter, when we 'die' . . ."

Looking bleakly to the past, I never really comprehended what any of these things truly meant. Like I say, Simon was the man with the knowledge . . .

"So your saying that my dream was Real . . . ?"

"Look man, who's there to tell you that it wasn't real. From the way you told your story, it must have seemed pretty real to you at the time . . . All those Real and Empathic Loving emotions that you felt!"

Affirmation was something so difficult to come by these days especially as all the different religions in the world Monopolise and separate . . .—Those that preach God as an outer being had obviously forgotten to have a conversation with Simon. These positive ideas seemed so logical now, and this was truly a turning point in my life . . . Life after Death, where God was your own inner entity . . .

"Simon, I love you brother. And now that you mention it—it seemed more real to me at the time than 99 percent of things in this state of consciousness, I was in tears as I wrapped my arms around her for the first time of meeting her properly again!"

Just the thought of my dream brought warmth to my heart. The empathic sentiment was allowed time to imbue the mind with positive thinking . . . With Loving sentiment, it seemed to me that Simon was a fallen angel that was trying to find his way home, and on his journey, he helped everyone along the way, whether they wanted his help or not . . .

"I mean all sorts of things have been associated with dreams . . . Freud founded some of his 'ideas' from the dream world. Some of his dreams were quite unfathomable however; where his father as the Centaur, castrated him as a boy—and as for the Oedipus Syndrome . . . Well . . . Wouldn't really like to ask him about that one! **His** Sub conscious finding cryptic ways of telling him things, this is a man that a lot of modern psychology is based on . . . It is obsolete and only serves as a thorn in the side of the Free thinker."

Simon pondered for a moment . . . "Should I mention that he was addicted to coke?"

Simon continued in a cool manner,

"I mean why do we have a sub-conscious of the mind, why isn't it all conscious!.?"

Simon's legendary speeches never ceased to impress, and on this occasion I was truly blown away, and he still hadn't finished!

"Do you know how I know this . . . ? Because everything in this state of consciousness is merely made up of a consolidation of atoms . . . Simple as condensed energy . . . even our own bodies! I have learned to become at peace with this fact, and because of it, I never get too worked up by it . . .—**Triviality**— . . . People are more my kind of game.

I go to the dream world every night and always have sweet dreams. I am pleasant to everyone I meet, tell them this is a dream and therefore the party can get started. I still, however, get the impression that the afterlife is a very dark place filled with unresolved issues and metaphorical demons . . . because yes, we all go to the same place when we die—regardless. It is my mission to clear this darkness up . . . It is in the dream world, that I am the enmity riddled' worst nightmare . . ."

Passing the joint my way again for the third time this morning, I could feel my eyes comfortably beginning to droop . . . I hadn't stayed up this early for a long time. Passing the joint Siobhan's direction, I coolly let out a second plume of smoke as I made myself Very comfortable in the enveloping beanbag. I was Loving every second . . .

"Goodness, I must be sounding as Crazy as that dude in craigers! I bet that they would love to take me away! Or maybe it's the parighuonoia setting in . . ."

DREAMER . . .

Standing in my silken robes before the steps of the senate arena, I hazily looked onward to the golden lightning rod pinnacle of the marble domed structure. Stain glassed windows beneath the dome burned soullessly as they glared outward over a jutting and pillared opening . . . the pillared and nauseating walkway that led to the Leviathan . . .

Objects shimmered in the darkness beneath a starry sky and sweat prickled on my furrowed brow and forearms. My distress worsened by the second. A knot of fearful anguish filled my being. With a gradual consuming darkness as my cover, I looked with blinding dread upon the grimacing and consuming formation . . .

I ran like the bitter wind that held fast to my tail . . . the terror began to tear a hole in my gut, never ending . . .

. . .

Stop.

Perfect clarity,

"I am dreaming . . ."

With sudden realisation I adhered to unspoken purpose. Unhindered, I consciously turned to face the distant pillar-like jaws of a taunting and mocking, immobile Goliath.

First of all flickering like a candle in the night, an encompassing and shimmering golden light emanated from my being. Looking to myself, I realised that my heart was shimmering with a golden light. This light began to grow and lit the way forward . . . Looking onward now at the darkened silhouette of shadow, I shook off my paralysis and ravaged closer with unrelenting fiery anger and determined endeavour . . .

Ever nearing with fearlessness as my companion, I slew ever closer with this unfolding light as it beamed to the pinnacle of the domed arena all the way to its base . . . With illumination, we were soon at One. Fervently looking around to the still darkened and desolate surrounding area with a tear in my eye, I tore at my chest and the entire universe was quickly enveloped with purifying light . . .

Out of nowhere and standing in admiration . . . Jade . . .

Waking, there was nothing but darkness. Realisation. True Enlightenment . . .

Waking again for the second time, I was accompanied by the smell of baking bread and distant conversation. Limbering up from my position from within the beanbag, I stretched to greet another morning. That smell of fresh bread . . .

Bumbling through the living room, I looked to the nostalgic grandfather clock that augmented the wall opposite the archway. It read 11.30am. On a mission to the kitchen, I comprehended the sub conscious dead weight of burden that was busying my mind.

—The flash back took me by the lapels

I looked upon myself, head in hands with delirium into the mirrored glass casing of the clock . . .

Like a flash, the illumination was quickly remembered, and my hands peacefully slipped away . . .

Continuing to the kitchen, the panic subsided just as quickly as it began. This moments madness shook me to my senses and a strange feeling of strength and worth filled my being. I had never before felt this way . . . Confidence was not the word . . . !

—Making my way through to the kitchen as One, the refreshed eyes of early morning company welcomed me to the breakfast bar that fruitfully partitioned the centre of the kitchen. The bright bowl as the centrepiece was overflowing, but one of the bananas in the bunch looked like it was beginning to turn . . .

A cheer arose,

"Morning sleepy head, thought you weren't going to see the morning!"

I stretched whole-heartedly with a confident and quirky smile . . .

"Ah you know I can't help it—your amazing ability to send people to sleep and all . . . You should consider getting a job as a sleep therapist or something . . . You did wonders for me!"

The 4 of us shared a chuckle to this private wit, as I headed to the breakfast bar with hungry intent.

"I take it you slept well then . . . ? We all headed off to bed pretty much straight after you fell asleep . . ."

The bags under Siobhan's eyes showed that she wasn't used to these all-nighters.

"We thought it best not to disturb you, seeing as you are in rather urgent need of some beauty sleep these days . . ."

The battle of droll between me and Psi never ceased until the balancing scales of our karmatic joking bond were evenly balanced, and then slightly tipped in favour . . .

"Enjoying our morning tea until the joker turns up . . ."

Rolling my eyes, I continued to acknowledge the three of them as I sat down and poured myself a glass of orange juice that was sitting on the side . . .

"What are your plans for this fine Saturday then Gabe . . . ?"

I looked out of the window to see that it was another over cast—but none the less—fine day . . .

"Haven't got anything planned to be truthfully honest, how about yourselves . . . ?"

Gulping down a large mouthful of fibrous cereal, Simon continued in a casual manner . . .

"Well you know the friend I was on about in craigers, I thought that we could go and visit him for the day if that's cool with you? . . ."

"Of course man, it would be good to meet the lad."

"We could head to the zoo!"

"Fair play, never would have pulled that out of the hat. Sounds like a good idea though! How about you two . . . ?"

I cast a gaze first of all to Siobhan and then to Mark as a brief silence was their only answer . . .

Siobhan looked to Mark,

"You seem a bit quiet this morning Mark, are you ok? Are you up for going . . . ?"

Silence Was again his only answer . . . Sleuthing from his position from under the spot light, he began to turn red and headed from the kitchen in the direction of the loo . . . Out of earshot, Simon spoke in a low voice . . .

"He was up for it last night, I almost had to put him in his place! I put it down to his consumption, but at his age, there are no excuses. He almost had his hands all over you! . . ."

"I know . . . If Lucifer was here he would have torn him apart! He got the message pretty quickly though . . ."

Out of friendship, Simon—respectful in all scenarios—stood his ground . . .

"He's only young, and we did have a fair bit last night . . ."

A few moments passed and Mark re-entered the kitchen with a beaming face. He knew his mistake, and judging from the silence, he could tell that I now knew the story . . .

I cast a gaze into the fruit bowl and decided to try and change the subject . . .

"Looking forward to seeing the apes myself, see how they operate as a flange . . ."

Changing the subject didn't work as Mark childishly cleared his throat. Following suit, I apishly fished out the turning banana. I made a ploy and relentlessly ate it without remorse . . . Mark briskly picked up his jacket and left without saying more than one word. Sorry.

"See you in college on Monday young Mark, don't be late . . . !"

The front door to the house slammed shut as he left . . .

Finishing my banana, I contemplated. Placing the skin into my empty cereal bowl, I drained the dregs of my mug of filtered coffee . . . Siobhan truly was the best host that has ever existed . . .

The fresh air gave the occasional welcoming breeze on this still day. There were pockets of blue sky that allowed the sun to shine through the thickets of grey, but despite the grey, there wasn't a black cloud in sight. A perfect day for the zoo! Looking to my watch, the timepiece read 1.10.

"Number 32 at 1.30 was what the timetable said . . . another 20 minutes to kill. It doesn't take too long to get to craigers from here."

The bus stop and surrounding area was devoid of any human activity, except for the occasional passers by who strolled casually by on the opposite side of the road. Rummaging in his pocket, Simon came packing and produced a pre-rolled joint. Looking to its tip as he sparked it up, he inhaled and held his breath . . .

"They should all be legalised man . . ."

I showed an intrigued but none the less naïve nod of agreement . . . After taking his second toke, he passed me the joint and looked at me as if he had a question on his lips . . . Blowing out a plume, he cleared his throat . . .

"Now Gabriel . . . I wonder, if in the fewest words possible, you could describe to me, in detail, what a drug actually is?"

A few moments of pondering passed, and I replied with the perfect answer . . .

"A chemical that stimulates a certain part of the brain, to release more of a certain type of chemical, that is naturally released anyway . . ."

Simon nodded his head in agreement . . .

"Not bad squire . . . I see that you have done a bit of research . . ."

Passing the joint my direction, I thoughtfully received and took a large toke. Letting out a plume of smoke . . .

"Not really bro, its just common sense, seeing as it is the truth and all . . . !"

Simon chuckled,

"Glad to see your open mindedness! Along with that natural part, you can also say that **all** chemicals are fundamentally natural when you think about it. I mean you have to ferment Demon Drink and that brings the worst out in all people, whereas marijuana—which chills everyone out and opens your mind to the possibilities of peace—grows naturally upon this planet . . . !"

Taking us by the hand, Psi saw fit to tell us the Undisputed Truth about all things in this modern day and present age, including drugs. We briefly used to touch on the subject, but this weekend seemed to be a full on learning point for us all . . .

"All these books, all this music and art that people hold close to their heart . . . 90% of this material is written when people achieve self realisation and enlightenment. It is my belief that drugs such as marijuana, help us to do this.

This world is full of blind hypocrites that haven't evolved since the dark ages. They see fit to judge another—more often than not, and generally anyway—by their choice to do drugs, as they go about their 'lives' Judging others with **their** closed minded, angry, naïve, immature and misguided condemnation."

Simon took a hapless breather, and briefly looked to the sky . . .

"Pandora's box . . . Do you know this tale . . . ?"

Simon looked at me with rhetoric . . .

"After being warned of the consequences of opening this box, Pandora 'foolishly' opens the box out of curiosity to see what secret lay waiting within. Demons of all kinds were released into the world and with all the darkness that takes president, a solitary butterfly is the very last entity to come out of the box . . ."

Spending a lot of my younger adult life with Simon, he sometimes brought up the satire of Pandora's box when talking about mental 'Illness'. Talking about how the demons of a mind may run amok and cause serious damage. Saying however that the butterfly showed that there was still beauty in the world and that there was hope that we could hope for a better future, just given a bit of time and consideration, time to make sense of things.

Demons that lay waiting within the mind.

"Psychiatrists in the 70s used to use LSD in their sessions. It used to give people the confidence and the key to unlock their Past or Face their Demons . . . It doesn't mess people up, it opens the Pandora's box of their mind . . . Now I have never taken acid—I Dream a more *natural* path—but I sure as hell don't point a condemning finger at those Individuals who choose to do it . . ."

Passing the joint back to Simon, I saw fit to keep the conversation going . . .

"How about all that stuff to do with taxation and the war on drugs that we used to talk about . . . ?"

Simon chuckled and looked to the floor as he spoke,

"Ah my young protégé, I'm glad to see that you Listen . . . !"

Sitting with his feet crossed and his arms in his lap, Simon changed his view to look to the unbiased middle distance. Taking a draw on his pre-rolled masterpiece, he coolly spoke.

"First off, Alcohol, Food and Nicotine are all drugs. I mean look at all these clinically obese people that are addicted to food—twinned with all those people who cant stop smoking . . . ! They are addicts!" Tapping some ash to the floor, "Nicotine does nothing for the brain, and is the most addictive drug there is, even more so than heroine, so I have been told . . . But of course what drugs are 'suitable' and those that 'aren't', has been drilled into everyone from the day they have been born by a hierarchy that decides what is 'best' for everyone . . . Making sure that we are kept in the *dark*, the news that we receive, is the news that they deem 'necessary' to *keep* people preoccupied and forever condemningly judgemental . . ."

Simon took a breather, and took another draw of Marijuana . . .

"The futile war on drugs costs the tax payer a lot of money, and fighting against an Individuals free right to do what they want . . . The ones that have a problem with this, are the gullible and cowardly flock that make up the majority of our populace . . ."

Simon cut to the point in a determined and unrelenting manner . . .

"Legalisation of all drugs . . .—Sounds crazy eh . . . Well guess what . . . Legalise all drugs, and guess what happens to drug crime . . . ? Do I have to spell it out any more . . . ? I mean the government brings in drugs anyway! As they buy it for pennies then sell it to the street cartells for profit. But think about all the money that would be saved by stopping the *futile* **war** on drugs, doubled with all the money that could be made from taxation . . . ! Wow, what a crazy suggestion. But of course, most are still glued to the horror stories that they see on TV, the insipid siphoned misinformation that keeps everyone blind . . . Triviality for those that don't have a life . . . Remember, everything in moderation . . ."

. . .

Looking at my watch as the humble timekeeper, I looked into the distance. A red double Decker bus could be seen heading towards us. As it neared, the number 32 could clearly be seen as it steadied along with the flow of moving traffic. Simon continued as the bus neared.

"Freud was a sad lonely old man addicted to Cocaine and even now in our present day, a lot of psychology is based on this man! It is **old** school mentality from the 30s. With everyone achieving some form of realisation, modern psychologists should start to Properly analyse what happens with the brain, rather than slapping a label on and forcefully medicating what they don't understand. I mean, how on earth is anyone supposed to get better, with this man as the psychologist! Surely they would get to his stage at best . . . ! People need to analyse Themselves Fully first, before they can go on a mission to help others . . . Freud was an onlooker . . ."

Flicking the joint to the floor, we paid our fare and traversed the stairs to the second story. Sitting together at the front of the half filled bus, I was soon vacantly looking out of the panoramic window to the flow of bumbling traffic.

5 minutes of quiet into the journey, an unspoken air of understanding kept us amused. Passing shopping complexes and sports-car forecourts, I uttered a rhetoric . . .

"Look at all that traffic man . . . All those cars that have one person driving them! . . ."

Breaking the quiet spell, Simons ears pricked as he turned to look out of the window to see the culprit of my condemnation . . .

After a brief period of watching the bumbling traffic,

"Driving is a luxury—especially these days with the rising price of fuel . . . All I hear about these days is people complaining about it"

A smile came to Simons face, as if I had just metaphorically hit the nail on the head . . .

"Not just the price of fuel, but the price of Everything! Consumerism is no longer the American dream, but of course, one day there will be blood money coming from different areas of the world. Can you guess where from?"

This last comment drew a few eyes in our direction as we comfortably sat on the bus. Simon was always keen to put the whole story across, especially if there was a disdaining audience . . .

"It is the undisputed truth that our western world of luxury is in recession. You know all about this Gabriel . . . ! Everything that is linked with recession leads directly back to Oil—and the banks hoarding away all the money in their vaults. Rather than putting the money to proper use and empowering the people, the banks lend out billions of dollars each year to the government so that more weapons of self-destruction can be produced to go to war with. But of course this money has to be paid back with interest, so how are we supposed to pay it back . . . the tax payer of course! Pretty soon, America will turn into a leper colony."

The two of us acknowledged the glaring onlookers with a smile. Simon continued . . .

"A warmongering—**Republican**—spokesman says that troops could stay in Iraq for the next 100 years . . . Can you imagine that.!? If so—can you imagine the reasons as to why this could be the case . . . ? Taking oil from the Saudi's rather than paying for it . . . Not a good move. It does not bode well for a placid and peaceful future with the rest of the world as different countries begin to unite . . ."

Being the core mission as the senate to stop these issues creating World War III, I knew this scenario inside out. On this occasion however, I was more than happy to listen to another one of Simons eloquent speeches. I was fed up of dealing with the spinning of the same old yarn . . .

Judging from my quiet stature, Simon continued.

"Now the war in Iraq **has** actually liberated the country from their fascist leader Sadamme, but in times like this, it is either the Democratic senate who shall rule—or Hussein's rule shall simply be replaced by that of the fascist and warmongering—Republican—Guidance *Front*. Ultimately, their goal intention was just to set up a precursor for stealing their oil, and if you think that terrorism is bad now!. They will tell you that it is liberation for the people, when ultimately, it is for their own personal—monetary gain! They want the oil."

Stopping at a set of traffic lights, I continued to look at the traffic and Animal Farm quickly sprang to my mind. Seeing people cough and splutter in the street, I looked to the Consumption and my anger began to burn . . .

"I mean they will go into Iraq—no problem. But other countries of the world that truly need liberation such as Zimbabwe, Libya and Syria, they are More than willing to turn a *blind* eye to. No personal gain there, they only see this as expense. It shows how little our hierarchy care for peace, or for any matter—human life . . . The entire wotld suffers, for the sake of a handful of 'people'—who want absolute power—and as always the have the majority of our populace' naïve acceptance of their warmongering ways! . . ."

The belligerent older people of the bus looked to Simon with a subtle—but none the less—hateful scorn. With no thought, they thought themselves important enough to be got at on a personal level, as if this 'taboo' subject was aimed solely at them.

Simon always used to tell me that one person, is not important enough to get worked up about and that it was time for everyone to grow up. The ones that were still looking to gratify their existence by looking to others, were the ones falling behind. Unperturbed, Simon happily continued . . .

"Coming back to our country and our life of luxury, people are more than willing to winge about the increase in **taxes** and cost of living, even though it is taxes that keep our economy functioning seeing as there is no help from the banks. They forget how good we have it in our western world . . . but saying that however, mental apathy, leading to reciprocated enmity, has bound and shackled almost everyone to the ground, this is accomplished without them even realising!"

Simon continued to ignore the contemptuous and poisoning gaze that he always seemed to attract . . .

"The western world and our life of luxury . . . They will even justify cardinal sin to sate their lust for wealth and power . . . Committing ultimate War crimes, yet no one sees a problem with this! The ones that are blind to this are the cowards that are more than happy to be herded around like sheep. Bahahhaa."

The scornful eyes that held nothing but contempt quickly subsided as Simon mocked with his witticism. Relaxing once again, we carried on our journey in peace. Our stop was just up ahead.

Thanking the driver and jumping off of the bus, I filled my lungs with welcoming, but none the less recycled—fresh air. The scornful and analysing eyes were soon forgotten as they were drearily driven off into the distance. Most likely travelling to another area that they would soon be contaminating their enmity riddled and rotten subconscious. Because yes, physical manifestations are a make up of what's going on inside the mind.

. . .

"Should give them something to think about . . . although saying that, even this is probably too much effort for them—let alone trying to do something about it! . . ."

The bus stop was a few minutes walk from the hospital. The autumn time of year brought to the ground every different shade of gold and brown, which left the pavement seemingly invisible beneath the camouflage of the once lush, now exposed, gnarled trees.

As if by using telepathy, Simon reassured me that it was the soundest state of mind which brought out the worst in everyone else. Like a subconscious magnet for enmity, as well as other physical manifestations brought on by unresolved mental issues. In this case, the enmity riddled stares that seemed to follow us as we walked on to Neil's ward.

Halfway down the main corridor, suits seemed to be looking down their noses. Under his breath as we continued onward,

"Pompous, arrogant succubus's . . . These suits earn their wages based on commission"

Simon continued to reassure me,

"These are the ones that twisted Neil's words and wrote notes about him that destroyed his hopes of a career with the RAF . . ."

LOONEY-BEEN

Dear Nan and Granddad,

Hello, how are you both? Sorry that I haven't been in touch sooner, have been feeling pretty down this last little while and haven't really been motivated to do much!

Sitting here day after day soon becomes a tedious affair. I didn't realise what boredom was until I came into this place. Have been here almost 3 months now, and it wouldn't surprise me if I have to spend a further 8 months here yet.

Looks like you were right about my crazy ideas one day getting me locked up Nan! **Crazy Time** eh—when you cant even talk about Peace without getting locked away, no questions asked . . .

At the end of the day, I have answered for all of the things that I have done in this life . . . I look back on my 'illness' as opening the Pandora's box of my mind. I now look back on it as the <u>ultimate</u> learning experience . . . I reflected on my past and learned to let it go. I no longer say that I lost my mind, instead, with my always positive attitude, I say that I found myself. My 'illness', taught me how to Love.

For some people, peace isn't enough. For those that 'live' in their own selfish and turmoil ed little world, they cant stand to see one who is free. They would rather try to *intervene* and start meddling in your life, than leave you be in peace and sort out their own shite. It quickly becomes very frustrating when everyone begins to point a finger at you, saying that you are ill . . .

First things first . . .

> A). Closed minded idiots, trying to tell **Me** how **I** am feeling . . .

And

> B). What I am entitled to believe according to the social standard of what is "Normal" . . . Booooring . . . I'd rather be myself than adhere to the whims of these suffocating automatons.

Instead of looking within themselves, these pompous bastards—Cos that's all they are . . . they think they're *better* than everyone else—psychoanalyse others in some naïve and desperate attempt to find some kind of resolve. Analysing other people with their retarded minds, polluting and punishing the ones that are free. I make them aware of their **own** inadequacies, and they don't like me for it. They are the ones that are riddled with anger—believe me . . .

They will look everywhere else, except with inside themselves. And so when iwas first of all dragged into this place against my will, I sat in a room with 6 other "gentlemen"—you know the ones that think they're better than everyone else—and I called them all a bunch of fucking cowards. The hostility was instantaneous . . . See, you're the ones with the problem, your getting angry right now . . .

With a silence and sudden realisation . . .

"Oh yeah" . . .

In the space of 5 seconds, all six of them just proved how feckless and childishly immature they all are. All of them apishly willing to take out **their** anger on someone else, especially the one telling them the undisputed truth. They do this in place of even beginning to fathom, what is really making them angry. They say that I'm ill, yet they cant even listen to the truth without getting angry. In their own closed minded and *consuming* egocentric State, I'm sure that they take great delight in having the Power to keep a young man—never having felt more alive—locked up.

They do a half assed job that the have 'learned' from obsolete psychiatry from the 1930s. Slapping a label on what they have no intention of even beginning to fathom or understand. If they were to actually listen to the ones that have been through it and put into practice the learned teachings of peace, everyone would see that there is no such thing as illness. They would soon be out of a job with this notion however and they would lose that little bit of power, which allows them to rule your life. They have not been through it, yet they swan around and harp on like they know it all! They know fuck all. You should try talking to someone who has been through it, and got better on their own . . .

I'm on medication at the moment, Quetiopiene. Their lame attempt to try and "Cure" me of my "condition". I cant even walk properly on the stuff . . . The only medication that works is people being there for you, who are truly willing to listen and talk some kind of sense back to you . . .

Anger was my last emotion to go and now that I'm not weighed down by that cowardly dead weight, I see it in everyone else and I seem to attract it like a subconscious magnet . . . Me and anger do not mix, yet my peaceful "Schizophrenic" mind, seems to rouse a latent hostility from others who are still willing to take their anger out on other people. I am a man that upholds the law of peace. I speak to people about the meaning of life, and through listening and talking the undisputed truth, I set you free . . . They say that I'm psychotic . . . All the negative connotations that go with that word . . . I wouldn't hurt a fly . . .

Anger manifests itself in many ways, and in place of **individuals** trying to resolve their **own** anger, they would rather pollute others with their own putrid enmity . . . Centring their emotions, answering for all that **they** have done and learning how to Love, seems to be below them. They are obviously too good for it and have risen above the need . . .

The only reason I went to see the psychologist was because I thought that my auntie Caz and uncle Dave had some talking to do. So the 4 of us (My cousin Matthew was there) sit in a room and after 20 minutes of silence, they start taking furniture out of the room. This is part to one of my poems and pretty much sums it up . . .

. . .

"What is your name . . . Where are you from . . . ?"

Was the derogatory demand, that slithered from his tongue.

My name is God brother, and I know all, including the outcome. Reiterating it makes me very tired, and quite simply, I answer to no-one.

Anger in his eyes, from such an "*arrogant*" quip—I liberate you all, so that you don't have to 'suffer' "his" egotistical whip.

"I have been hearing from others that you aren't yourself . . ."

. . . I look into your soul, and then look to my right. The enmity and anger polluting the air is all the proof I need, for the fact that **I** am fine.

20 minutes of silence, with everyone reflecting. Peace. I suppose that this is the justification, for calling the police.

My lack of cooperation with this parasites interrogation, led to the inevitable—against my will 'condescending' injection. Refusing to back down, I peacefully stood my ground, and it took 7 of you fuckers, to restrain a peaceful man. 3 times that fucking hand cuff was wrought round my arm, and there was me thinking the police were there to keep people from harm.

Putting a needle in my arse, why don't you pucker up and kiss it . . . You make me laugh. I look to my wrist and I look to the mark, just another peaceful battle scar. Oh shit, almost forgot my family . . . they don't just have the cheek to stand and stare, they smile at the manifestation of their own despair. After restraining me physically, you rejoice with glee, tears from my cousin Matthew as he is one who is free.

Police officers, "We're doing *nothing*" Except upholding the law . . . How about that one along the lines of Freedom of speech you whore For all of you who still adhere to their infectious notion, you are the ones that need the injection.

So now I'm in here, the most relaxed man in the ward, taking medication to relax me . . . It makes me wonder what other manifestations, I have to look forward . . .

. . .

After 7 of them restrained me, I'm sitting down. My uncle Dave walks back into the room after the "commotion" and doesn't even look at me. Instead, he starts smiling as he tries to worm his way into the exclusive crowd of ego junkies. Before the commotion, during our 2 minutes of reflection, he looked almost dead. My auntie Caz was twittering away with some pathetic triviality that was really starting to annoy me. I properly drilled it into them that they had some reflection to do rather than leaving the task for someone else to do.

I have learned how to Love, even after All the shit that has happened, therefore I am no longer 'ill'. It's all those other fuckers out there that try to tell you how to live your life and what you should and shouldn't be thinking. They are the "ones" who are truly fucked up, and they will happily continue to hinder everyone else that they come across thinking in some way that looking down their nose at people, earns them respect . . . Their want of being thought of as superior. They will probably suffer this egotistical affliction and pollute others with their sickness for the rest of their sorry excuse and sham—which they class as a life . . . In my mind, the after life has a nice cell waiting for them. A place where we will all be free, away from **their** contaminating mentality . . .

Just a crazy mans ramblings at the end of the day eh . . . Sweep me under the carpet and outcast me like all those other crazy people out there . . . Well . . . that's what they would like to do, but I'm pretty sure that the peaceful people of the world shall soon begin to stand up against the bullies of the world . . .

I don't need the angry weight of burden to be the ruthless and Loving man that I am today.

I shall write again soon, all my Love,

Neil.

—

"You alright Neil, how are you getting on man? Few months no see, how are you keeping? I take it they're treating you properly in this place?"

"Oh you know how it is man," came the mans peaceful tone, "Just the usual, same shit different day, good to see you again Psi, who is this your with?"

"This is my good friend Gabriel! He is one of the main senate speakers. You may recognise him from TV?"

Moving to one of the free chairs in the hazy smoking room, I sat down and took in the surroundings. Magnolia walls fifteen feet square moulded into shaded green potted plants that stood about 5 feet tall, as bright sunshine, shining through a break in the cloud, shone through sturdy security windows.

Neil and Psi followed suit and took a seat.

"Oh aye, now you mention it he does look a little familiar. So you're the voice of the people?" Neil asked in an excited tone. "So being almost at the top Gabriel, what dirt do you have on the opposition?"

Simon smiled to himself as he left an excited Neil to speculate as I was left on the spot.

"Well they keep their secrets pretty firmly hidden away, mistakes are erased and monumental conspiracies are covered up with ease. It sometimes makes me wonder how it's done . . ."

"By use of the media, my dear friend. The National Guidance **Front** has them n their pocket and the news we receive is the siphoned misinformation that keeps everyone in the dark. You have to search for the real news and what's truly going on . . ."

Neil's highlander accent grabbed my attention,

"Like does it ever make you wonder how banks make their money?"

Thinking back to when Simon was talking about production of weapons and self destruction,

"Yeah they lend it to the government, who then pay it back with interest . . ."

"Ahh, I see you have been doing some research! Good stuff, you shall save me a breath. Yes the production of weapons . . . Billions of dollars a year that the government borrows from the bank. In times of war, this borrowing of money greatly increases, hence more money for the banker as the government pay back the money with added interest!"

"Production of weapons" Psi interjected, "It makes you wonder why the war in Vietnam lasted so long. Of course, this makes sense when thought of, the longer that arms and munitions need to be produced, the more money needs to be borrowed from the banks . . . Makes some people very wealthy indeed, mainly the rockerfellers and roosevelts."

Neil considered this for a moment and talked through his hands as if in prayer,

"All those lives that were lost . . .

It was later found out that the sinking of the two destroyers responsible for the war weren't actually destroyed by Vietnam PT boats. The captains were furious at propagandas ignition for the war . . ."

"So your saying that the war was started over nothing?"

"That's right, nothing but monetary gain for the banks . . ."

"Wow, that's news to me . . ."

"Well have you heard of the true terrorists of the world? That's right, the western world. Were you aware that 9-11 was a inside job? The day the twin towers were hit, Dick Chaney was orchestrating war exercises in a bunker beneath the white house. This sent false readings to NORADS radars. They couldn't distinguish between real world or exercise. This was so that a new anti terrorist legislation could be enforced it would also fan the flames of hatred towards the Middle East. They needed a certain amount of deaths before this was allowed to pass."

Unhindered, we walked in companionship to the sound of distant human and animal activity . . . Above all the noise, one particular screech could be heard above all of the others as we neared the main entrance . . .

"Sounds like your mating call Gabriel . . ."

Sharing a chuckle, I relaxed and made a comeback . . .

"Nah man—that's their alarm bell ringing . . . They can sense your presence!. They know there's no escape . . ."

Never ceasing, we continued with light hearted banter up to the ticket office . . . The sign read £18 for adults and £12 for children and OAP's.

"It must be your lucky day Psi . . . You even get into the place at a reduced rate . . . !"

Never one to be beaten, Psi always had a comeback . . .

"Yeah well that's because you weren't able to read the part of the sign that said carers also get in for £12!"

Neil was the level headed and caring peacekeeper among the three of us

"The way you two are carrying on you both should be allowed in for £12! Anyhoo you two . . . I'm the one looking after the both of you . . . I have my eye on you . . . !"

Me and Psi both sensed that an immediate change of discussion was needed.

"£18 each . . . Goodness—we must be living a life of luxury!"

Paying our way through the ticket office, we were immediately surrounded by childish laughter and grown ups shouting at their children to behave. Hordes of people could be seen feeding animals and filling their own faces with beef burgers . . . Siding to the souvenir shop to the right of the entrance, Neil purchased a map . . .

"Goodness, you even have to pay for the map!"

After the commotion, the three of us huddled together around the map and decided where to go first. Looking to the map, the monkey and ape enclosure was the third section of the zoo heading in a clockwise direction.

With the sun shining through a break in the cloud cover, we happily basked in reptilian territory for a while. Soon heading onward, the creepy crawly sanctuary was just up ahead. We were soon on our way . . .

"Rah"

Lightly grabbing Neil by the shoulders, I gave him a slight but firm jolt. Positively crapping himself as he looked with horror into the Perspex containers of a tarantula enclosure. He spun on his heel only to be faced with that of the funnel web spider. He quickly and quietly made his way back to the entrance.

A cover up of the 1st degree, as even I was on edge on this particular expedition. Uneasy, but none the less fascinated. Simon appeared to be in his element.

"Look at that bro . . ."

Simon was eyeball to Perspex as he looked with fascination to a tarantula making a meal out of a petrified cricket . . . with satirical wisdom, Simon spoke as if diagnosing a prognosis . . .

"Thickness for thickness, apparently spider web has a higher tensile strength than iron! Hence to say that there's no escape for the poor blighters being dropped to their doom. Only being bred for food, what an existence . . ."

Slowly moving along, I looked onward with uneasy tension as the zookeeper lifted the lid on another casing. On edge, we soon arrived at the doorstep of the gargantuan bird-eating spider.

I could no longer bare the sight . . . I too span on my heel, and decided to leave before I began to have nightmares . . .

"Just gonna see how Neil is . . . keep him company for a bit . . ."

Simon looked up from his reflection and nodded his head . . .

"So that's your excuse you wuss . . . I take it that your not up for seeing whether we can hold one of the tarantulas then no . . . ?"

Simons dry bedside manner did little to nurse my phobia and I was soon hairily walking through a crowd of people back out of the entrance. Neil was there to greet me with a whimsical and cheeky smile . . .

"Started getting to you after a while as well then eh . . . ?"

Shaking off my crawling skin, I gave a dry smile of acknowledgement and put a finger to my lips . . .

"Shhhh . . ."

Again Neil smiled . . .

"Or was it something simple like Simons company that caused you to flee . . . ?"

Giving this comment a moment of thought, I thought back to how fearful these creepy crawlies made me feel. I quickly cut in . . .

"His company is spot on . . . but that mutha of a bird eating spider was something else! . . ."

The thought of the elongated and hairy legs made my skin crawl. I quickly changed the subject to steer my mind to less intrusive thoughts . . .

A few minutes of banter passed and Simon emerged confidently and triumphantly from a bustling crowd of people. Fresh faced and eager, he strolled up to the two of us in a self assured manner,

"You two are wimps . . . ! You know that they wont be able to touch you from behind that Perspex . . ."

Standing to his usual enigmatic pose, Simon carried on with a slight seriousness to his tone . . .

"Even if they could touch you, all you have to do is stay relaxed . . . Apparently they can sense your fear . . . There is nothing to be afraid of! You two really did deserve to get in at a reduced rate!"

Simons half serious approach to our cowardliness cut through the fearful webbing of our mind as his sentiment rang true. Even this slight sentiment taught me a lesson, as it wasn't only spiders that could sense our anxiety . . .

"Fear manifests itself in many ways and if you wish to be free from this dead weight of burden—you need to learn how to stay relaxed at **All** times, that means you are halfway there, to the path of true enlightenment . . . Gabriel . . . you in particular have to have a will stronger than steel . . . A proposition is awaiting you that requires unhindered and fervent ability, don't worry me with the thought that you aren't the man for the job, as there is no other man! Remember that proposition I mentioned . . . ?"

I looked to Simon with puzzlement. The thought was already there, but now I knew that there was something he wasn't telling me. Continuing to the ape enclosure in a mutual quiet, I was about to ask in a serious manner—but before I had a chance to speak, Simon cut in . . .

"We are heading to Lucifer's club tonight. And if you can believe it, you are the guest of honour! Your position in the senate has kindled an interest . . . Be patient Gabriel, as all shall be revealed later this evening . . ."

We continued to the enclosure in silence.

The alpha male of the group could be seen straight away. He was the biggest and boldest of the group and was a waking slumber in his tree-like throne. The rest of the male company revered his position with a slight submissiveness and he was surrounded on all sides by females.

The massive Perspex enclosure made sure that no-one got their fingers pulled off, and photographers all around us were busy snapping shots of the communal family household.

Holding the biggest banana in the group, the alpha male sat comfortably with the rest of his family as they peacefully went about their business. Play fighting still ensued with the younger males of the group, but they were kept a close eye on by both the alpha males and other females. Neil giggled and his contagion soon had the rest of us chuckling . . .

"Look at that perfect and peaceful family circle . . . Unhindered by all of our eyes."

We looked on with respect at the ordered and peaceful family unit. I thought to myself how worked up they may get if they were threatened by another family or straying Individual.

Simon wistfully spoke up . . .

"Seems to be more peaceful than most of the family life that I hear about these days!"

This truth rang through the three of us and the rest of the families that surrounded, looked upon Simon with regard . . . Simon changed his view to looking directly at the dominant male. Their eyes soon met, and Simon did not look away . . .

Limbering up from his peaceful slumber, the chief of the group stood upright and glared directly at Simons provoking eyes. Standing tall, the getile giant began to thump his chest and let out an almighty roar. The others in the group showed immediate and submissive attention.

Simon continued to eyeball the encaged beast, but realising the Perspex, the ape soon relented and calmed back to his previous and unrelenting slumber. The rest of the flange, realising the culprit of the uproar, ignored and also continued to go about their business.

Forever making a point, Simon turned his attention back from eyeballing the beast and set his eyes upon us . . . but before he had a chance to speak, I jumped in . . .

"Well you sure did a good job of winding that ape up, all you had to do was look at him . . . ! Saying that though, I'm not surprised he was offended!"

The surrounding family members shared an out-casting snigger that had Simon on the spot . . . Simon was never a man to be outdone and so out of nowhere he raised his arms above, let out an almighty roar and banged his chest for the whole zoo to hear!

A coupe of photographers snapped a quick shot, and a few seconds of astounded silence passed . . .

"Pretty good impression to!"

Smiles and laughter followed as Psi took a bow to the crowd. After recovering from the media rabble, Simon gave a sly and jaunted wink in my direction and in a hushed tone,

"Told you man, intricate workings . . ."

Leaving the family unit to their own devices, we headed away from the enclosure with a light heart and confidence as our companion.

Remembering the scene, I thought back to how Simon dealt with being on the spot. He truly was a confident man . . . In appreciation of his deed, I playfully spoke,

"That was quite a spectacle back there, you handled it well . . . Again I'm impressed!"

Simon smiled to the floor and Neil spoke in delight . . .

"Just goes to show that even Looking at that ape the wrong way was enough of a provocation . . . You would have been screwed if that Perspex wasn't there to protect you!"

Simon spoke with seriousness,

"Well I sure wouldn't have provoked him if we were in the wild—he has the strength to tear you limb from limb! Thought I would make a statement though, the point being that their system operates by something simple as body language!"

Simons true recovery soon had me and Neil looking to the floor . . .

"We read body language since the day we are born and the ones that think they are clever by reading it, have clearly forgotten to look at themselves."

Simon looked over his shoulder to catch a distant glimpse of the caged beast. Turning again to face us . . .

"The day that people stop looking to other's body language for answers, is the day that people start to see things from a new perspective. People are always willing to analyse other people's virtues with a conceited and jealous eye as unaware, they go about their life naively resorting to this Consuming Neanderthal tactic"

. . .

"When they stop scrutinising others, they may learn how to Listen and Empathise with people, rather than holding dear to the prejudice which has been taught to them from day one. When they grow up and look to **Find Themselves**, they should start to realise that it doesn't matter what people look like, it is the heart and mind that makes a person and not the clothes that they wear."

Simon continued in an inspiring manner,

"I was serious when I said you need to have a will stronger tan cold steel Gabriel. A few words do so much more damage than a sword could ever do . . ."

The time was around 5pm and the weather remained unchanged. Making our way back through the entrance of the zoo, we decided what was next on the agenda . . . Neil was the first to speak up,

"What now then gents?"

A silence fell among the three of us but Simon quickly broke the spell . . .

"Well that was an awesome Friday and Saturday and I look forward to this evening too! Next on the agenda for me is getting back home to take a shower and get ready for this evening . . ."

Again a look of bemusement came to my face . . . Psi quickly spoke up,

"Lucifer says to be at his club for 11. He's sending a limousine to come and pick us up at 10! We have been invited round to Siobhan's for about 9 this evening if you want to come along . . . ?"

Feeling slightly sorry for Neil as he had to go back to the hospital, I spoke in a slightly disgruntled manner.

"Well if I knew what the plan was then I might know how to dress . . ."

Simon smiled as if no matter what I said, he wasn't sifting on the information front . . .

"Ahh my eager younger brother" Simon quipped . . . "I aint giving anything away . . . you shall just have to be patient and wait until later this evening!. Casual and smart dress should do the trick, remember, you're the guest of honour, so you cant be in a bad mood on an occasion like this!"

Looking to the ground, I chipped a small stone in a side tracked notion . . .

"I know my way to Siobhan's, 9 o clock sounds like a good time . . ."

Just as Simon and Neil were about to make a move back to the hospital Simon pulled out his wallet. Producing a folded sheet of paper, he placed it into my hand with a smile . . .

"You are also allowed to invite a guest and I'm sure that Jade would be more than happy to keep you company!"

I looked at the neatly hand written number with a kiss at the end of it. Dumfounded, my heart missed a beat and I felt butterflies as I remembered her beauty. I quickly folded the paper in half and put it in my pocket and thanked Simon for his sly deed with a wry smile. Saying farewell to the two of them, I made a solitary mission back to the bus stop . . .

Sitting patiently, I waited for the bus in contemplation. My mind cast back with an open view of the past 24 hours and my brain began to digest. Silently piecing all of it together, I now noticed how a few of the Vacant eyes which cast their gaze in my direction showed unprovoked hostility. Not finding this particularly unusual however, I ignored them and silently acknowledged the more mature and peaceful members of society . . . With my bus coming into clear sight, I was soon on my way . . .

HOME . . .

The 20 minute bus journey was a relaxing comfort. Surveying the area again with an insightful and panoramic view, I looked onward to the bustling crowds and rabble of "Individuals" that lugged around large quantities of designer shopping bags. I thought to myself, how much would they have to say if I was ever to speak to them . . .

Melodrama and Triviality . . .

My stop was a 5 minute walk away from home. Thinking of all the closed minded and blind suburbanites that I was on a mission to help, I now realised how consumed and wrapped up they were in their own little world to care for anyone else . . . Bringing around a feeling of lonely nostalgia, I continued home with powerless turmoil as my companion, what was I to do. Passing a homeless man on the street begging me for change, I realised how much our own country was in a state, let alone the rest of the world . . .

Reaching my front door did a little to lift my spirit. My feline companion Jasper came out of nowhere and brushed around my legs . . . He wasn't the only one who was hungry . . . entering my front door, I found a small pile of envelopes that looked official, but were none the less junk mail . . . More bureaucracy . . .

The kitchen was my first port of call,

"Meow"

After feeding Jasper his usual meaty treat, I prepared myself a legendary salad sandwich and took my time over the triple decker veggie delight . . . After wiping my chops, I headed to the shower and washed my dark brown shoulder length locks and rinsed away the weekends' film of grime . . .

The shower did wonders for lifting my mood. Getting changed into a smart pair of trousers and shirt, I fished out the folded piece of paper from the pocket of my suit trousers and placed it on the counter in the kitchen. A few moments of confidence building passed and I soon picked up the phone . . . a couple of rings passed and the phone was soon lifted at the other end . . .

"Hello . . ."

Preparing for the dive . . .

"You alright Jade . . . ? It's Gabriel from the other night . . . Remember . . . ?"

Eagerly awaiting a response, Jade quickly replied,

"Gabriel! Of course!. How could I forget, how are you!?"

"Good thanks yeah . . . How are you today, are you well . . . ?"

"Yeah good as well thanks . . . I have the next 2 days off work, so I'm having a good time kicking back and relaxing away from the local! Glad to hear that you got my number ok."

Chuckling to myself, I remembered Simon and his sly deed . . .

"How would you feel about coming out with me this evening . . . ? There are a group of us heading to one of Simon's friends clubs tonight. Apparently I'm the guest of honour if you can believe that?! Just wondering if your up for coming as a VIP . . . ?"

"VIP!. Yeah, sounds like a great idea! Simon told me a little about it when we realised that you drifted away from our conversation . . . Soul yeah . . . ?"

"Soul . . . ?"

"Yeah that's the name of the club we're heading to tonight . . ."

Tutting under my breath to the notion that Jade knew more about the evening than me,

"Fair play . . . So are you up for it then . . . ?"

"Well I have already washed my hair, so . . ."

Crossing my fingers had worked . . .

"52 High Broadway. Be there for 9.00 . . ."

Hanging up the phone, I excitedly smiled to myself. I couldn't wait for this evening. Realising that there was another 3 hours to kill, I rolled myself a joint, and picked up the guitar . . .

The Voice of Reason

The time was 8.30 and being a man of good time keeping, I planned on arriving at Siobhan's place for just before 9. Heading to the door, I said my farewells to Jasper and jumped in the taxi that was waiting outside . . .

Jumping into the front seat . . .

"Where you heading to bruv? . . ."

The middle aged cockney accent was a familiarity that I had become accustomed to after spending 6 years of my life here.

"52 High Broadway . . ."

After pulling away, the taxi driver gave me a good once over.

"You look familiar bruv. I'm sure that I've seen you somewhere before . . ."

Always happy to talk, I had time for everyone who was pleasant enough for a mutually respecting conversation . . .

"Do you follow politics at all my friend . . . ?"

Changing gear,

"Ahh . . . I recognise you now . . . you're a member of the senate aren't you . . . ? The voice of the people and what not . . ."

"That's right bro, the voice of the People . . ."

Stopping at a red light, the driver looked at the other surrounding vehicles.

"What do you think of our opposing voice? . . ."

A few seconds passed as the driver pulled away . . .

"You mean the Guidance **Front** . . . ? Man, don't get me started on that one . . . Are you on about past, present or the future of these fuckers . . . ?"

"Start anywhere you like bro,—your ramblings will be sweet music to my ears . . ."

Me and the driver shared a chuckle as the fragile territory we were treading was smashed as it showed signs of cracking beneath our feet . . .

"Freedom of speech and the like . . . I remember, was it yesterday that I saw you on live comm? Man that pissed me off. Cutting you down like that in the middle of your speech!"

I hung my head as the thought of my powerless voice re-emerged . . .

". . . Do you remember how they brought their way into power a couple of years back . . . ? With all of the political parties in disarray, a new party of super rich Oil Barons promised renewed economy and welfare for *our* people. All that the public had to do was sign over their Soul and vote for the guidance front in the last election. They are now the ones who hold a monopoly of power and money in our western world! . . ."

The driver was busy concentrating on what he was doing, but I could tell he was enthused by our conversation . . .

"It was the political backbenchers who saw he reality behind their corrupt dealings and so the opposing senate was formed. Their fascist doctrine means that they are free to do as they please for at least the next 2 years, unhindered . . . They justify their executive—warmongering decisions by saying that it is what is best for **our** people."

The driver gave me a brief look of acknowledgement. I continued in a relaxed manner . . .

"En masse, the duped and naïve public gladly eat up this fallacy with blind greed as they go about their day consuming and taking everything for granted. The ones that *'listen'* to the misleading and rhetorical speeches that take them as gospel as they fall on deaf ears and blind eyes . . . Not caring for the troubles of the real world is how people pay their *owners* in kind for the western worlds fucked up condition, as 99% of us are **kept** *'happy'*, so long as our lust for money and consumer products is sated . . ."

Clearing his throat, the driver replied in a cultured manner . . .

"Now you mention it bro, I wasn't aware that they were oil tycoons . . . I have never really been a true follower of politics but I must say that your logical outlook has already taught me a lesson . . . I just jumped on the band-wagon when I cast my vote in their favour . . ."

Realising sense, the driver looked slightly ashamed as if he had just realised the true mentality of the divide between peace and war . . . I tentatively joked with a light hearted tone . . .

"Don't worry bro . . . You weren't the only one!"

Chuckling to myself, the driver soon broke a smile . . . I soon continued . . .

"The only reason as to why the senate are not in power is because with our intention, the western world would feel the full effects of recession. This is because there would be no other **subsidies** supporting our country, other than that of the hard working tax payer . . . This is because the bankers are hoarding all of the money. When the government is in financial worry, no one is there for them. When the banks are in trouble, the government bails them out . . . If only there were some kind of subsidy . . ."

A moment of respectful silence passed as we stopped again at another set of lights . . .

"It is times like these that we all have to stand together brother, rather than adhere to the separation that has always been taught to us . . . We have to realise that there is more to life than just money . . . the human race is Our agenda . . ."

Out of nowhere, the man suddenly seethed as if I had said something wrong . . .

"Money and separation . . . Tell me about that one bro . . .—I have an ex-wife who stole three of my kids away from me!. One day, after the shortest legal battle known to Man, left me behind as she swanned in and took the three of my children away 'all' questions asked! I looked after them for 6 long years and now only see them twice a week! I even have to pay that bitch child support!"

Pulling away from the lights, I thought of some way to recoil the slight awkwardness that I had awoken . . .

"One of the many issues that we deal with as the senate . . . The national guidance front do not care for your or mine welfare, they only care for their own wealth and Power . . . If you want someone to blame, point a middle finger at them by voting for the senate in the upcoming election . . . try to convince as many people as you can . . ."

The man chuckled as we stopped on the road opposite the ivy-trimmed house . . .

"You put across a good argument my friend . . . I shall have to keep my eyes open for your truths when I watch more often. Thanks bro . . . Keep your head held high . . ."

"Cheers bro, same to yourself . . . There's a 20 . . . Keep the change."

. . .

Coolly jumping from the taxi, I was immediately harangued by a bitter and constant wind that chilled my loosely clothed body . . . Standing beneath a cloudless and starry night sky, I took a breath of cool air and waved to the driver as he pulled away. Crossing the road, I thought back to our conversation. Drowned by the rabble of everyday thought brought around a feeling of virtual obsolescence that hung like a weighty knot around my neck . . .

My humbled feeling was thoughtfully gratified as I reached the gate. The thought was, that so long as everyone had the same naïve attitude toward life, things were never going to change . . .

With the taxi out of view, I crossed the road and headed up the 20 foot garden path to the house. A different atmosphere surrounded the house this night, but it still held true to its warm and welcoming stature. Arriving at the doorstep, I knocked on the sturdy oak door . . .

Taken aback for a second by Siobhan's alluring beauty, I met her splendour and sparkling eyes with a smile. A welcoming warmth enveloped my being . . .

"Wow . . . You look stunning!"

With a sentimental chuckle . . .

"Thanks Gabriel, come in . . . !"

Walking through the door, I past by her aura of beauty and smelled the scent of sweet perfume . . . Glad to be in the warmth of company, I quickly shook off my ill feeling and adjusted to the ambient and peaceful surroundings of a loving home. The door clicked shut and Siobhan turned to face me with a grin,

"Don't let my husband catch you saying that!"

Smiling away, Siobhan led the way to the kitchen and playfully shimmied as she walked . . .

"The others should be here shortly, would you like a glass of wine?"

"Yeah a glass would be great!"

Reaching into a tanned oak cupboard, Siobhan produced a couple of glasses . . . Filling a glass,

"So are you looking forward to this evening then Gabriel . . . ?"

I was in two minds about the evening. On one hand there was the thought of clubbing until the early hours and in the other, was the wondrous intrigue as to what the evening was all about.

"Yeah tonight should be great fun . . . I haven't been clubbing in ages! Must say though that I'm waiting with wondrous intrigue to find out what the evening is all about!"

With a hinting tone to my voice,

"I'm quite looking forward to finding out what this proposition is about! . . ."

After filling the second glass, Siobhan put the half filled bottle on the breakfast bar and headed to the far end of the kitchen. Not catching the hint . . .

"I take it you have told to keep shtum about this evening as well then . . . ?"

With glass in hand, Siobhan placed a cd into the surround sound hi-fi and tinkered with the buttons.

"To be honest Gabriel, I am about as clued up as you are as to what this evening holds in store! Lucifer keeps a firm divide between his working and home life."

Siobhan returned from the far end of the kitchen to the opening and melodious riff to 'love is a stranger'. At that exact moment, there was a sudden knock at the door . . .

"That should be them!"

. . .

Solitary for a moment, I stood waiting in anticipation. A brief moment of excitement passed as butterflies filled my stomach . . . Taking a large mouthful of wine, I cleared my throat in an attempt to try and calm my slight nervousness . . .

Siobhan opened the door . . .

"Simon how are you . . . ?"

"Good thanks yeah . . . ! This is to make up for the other night . . ."

A wedding ring finger clinked around a bottle of wine,

"You must be Jade?! Welcome, please come in! . . ."

Taking another mouthful of wine, the door clicked shut.

"Let me take your coats . . . Head on through to the kitchen, Gabriel is here."

Entering through into the kitchen first was a very smartly dressed Simon. A fitting tuxedo and smart shoes . . .

"Wow . . . Very smart Simon! You scrub up rather well!"

Quickly blending in with the warm surroundings,

"Cheers bro, you don't look half bad yourself!"

In a hushed tone

"Wait til you see Jade . . ."

Shimmying back into the kitchen, Siobhan walked to the breakfast bar.

Jade . . .

. . .

An air of splendour entered into the kitchen as the archetype of beauty glided into the kitchen as an hourglass figure. With a black dress flowing freely over her curvaceously toned body. Jades brunette locks bounced freely as they curled buoyantly at the ends. With sparkling brown eyes that truly beamed, a breath of mine was taken away as the windows to our Soul soon met . . . With red voluptuous lips surrounding a set of pristine pearly whites, I welcomed in admiration with a kiss to her perfectly smooth skin.

The tension immediately subsided and gave way to a heart warming sensation . . . Wow . . . What a smile.

Taking in this heavenly sight, Siobhan reached into the cupboard and produced another couple of glasses, Psi opened his bottle and re filled all of our glasses. With drinks in hand, we clinked glasses and shared a cheers,

"For Peace . . ."

For peace.

Leading onward to the living room, Siobhan stopped about a third of the way up the hallway. Out of a dozen or so pictures, she ushered us to look at one in particular.

The Climax of Battle . . . Fighting through blood red flames with shield and sword in hand, St. George looked as though he was just about to thrust his tool through the jade and crimson scales that protected the dragon's heart . . .

After a few moments of taking in the work of art . . .

"Lucifer always liked this one in particular. He says that the dragon represents our fascist Hierarchy, and that St. George was the only man—the Sole knight—who had the courage to face and slay evil and corruption however it chose to manifest itself . . ."

Leading on through to the main room, I looked onward at the other works that were lit up by individual shaded lamps. Entering again into the vast living room a couple of minutes after the others, I commented on the artwork that struck an empathic chord in my heart . . .

"That's quite a display you have there . . . The one with the coiled python and the petrified rabbit is also a powerful satire . . . Where on earth do you find such works of art.?"

"Lucifer is the collector . . . He knows a lot of people who know people through his business. If your rich enough and have an interest in art, its surprising how many down to earth people you can meet. There is a story behind every painting . . . Lucifer shall have to guide you around them all at some point!"

Simon spoke in an inquisitive manner.

"So which one are you Gabriel, the rabbit or St. George . . . ?"

Lost for words, I looked to the floor . . .

Jade came to my rescue,

"I would say that I feel more of a heroic Olympian vibe myself. One with a deep sense of determined and dogged resolve . . ."

Looking to Jade, I gave a thankful and appreciative smile. The 4 of us shared a chuckle . . .

"There we go Psi, how's that? So which one are you . . . ?"

"Me!?" Simon started, "I'm more of the stoic observer and shepherd to the light! No glamour with me except for the extremely sharp wit and clarity which you have come to know . . ."

Siobhan spoke up,

"Well I'm sure that your wit would almost certainly have cut the dragons head clean off . . . So much so that wasn't it your forked tongue that got you sacked by the senate.?"

Simon recoiled as if he had just been assaulted for inciting bad taste against my character . . . but the true reason for such an assault ran even deeper . . .

"Look . . . I'm not starting an argument! And it sure isn't my fault that the other senators have no sense of humour . . . !" Simon was stern for a moment . . . "And I wasn't sacked, I resigned remember . . . !"

Casting a glimpse back with the eye of my mind, I looked to Simon with a nostalgic and beginning of hilarity kind of smile . . .

"Yes . . . Sense of humour . . ."

Simon spoke in a delight of self defence . . .

"Well it sure isn't my fault that the guidance front lack the ability to satisfy their wives . . . All those meetings where there are desperate housewives abound, you know how it works!"

The four of us laughed . . .

"How many of them did you bed in the end . . . ?"

"Enough to have caused an uproar. Four . . . That was before my *wild* wife tamed me."

. . .

Remembering the deed and the consequences brought around a hilarity that was edged with seriousness . . .

"I'm surprised that you don't have a number on your head after a dealing like that . . ."

Unperturbed, Simon coolly took a mouthful of wine and drank in admiration of his one-man mission, heroic deed . . .

"Oh the numbers definitely there brother, just not the one your thinking of! When it comes to women, I just couldn't help myself!"

Simon was, at the time, young and reckless and in his first few months as a senator he was already notorious . . .

"What time is the limo picking us up? . . ."

Corporate giant—Lucifer Grey, had a theory about Life. Soul was the latest trend to hit the streets of London, and was one of the greatest chains of clubs and casinos to ever arrive on the scene. It was also rumoured the owner and true Liberator, was allegedly the lead developer in the condemned and 'notorious', narcotics trade.

Rising from the depths—compared to what psychologists and sociologists of the age classed as 'normal'—allowed this Individual to shine whole-heartedly from the shadows. Forever thinking, was a mind that was able to see everything for what it truly was. A mind that was able to realise the true value and potential of anyone or anything that came his way. Revelations to human potential, led to an untapped and open gap in the market and for the first time in 'history', was the chance to open the eyes of all who were willing to listen. With pure intention, he endeavoured to achieve mass Enlightenment, with the aspiration to <u>help</u> create an understanding and peaceful new era. This was soon to be born . . . But shaking the foundations of a totalitarian ruled society, is not taken too kindly by the powers that be. Something had to be done, and the perfect opportunity, was just about to step into his office.

After popping a bottle of champagne, we jumped from the limousine and the tinted windows rolled off into the distance. The grandeur entrance to the club was home to a couple of burly men who stood at a queue of about 200 people. Bustling with people beneath the glowing neon sign, Soul.

Strolling up to the two finely dressed gentlemen, I reached into my pocket and produced the sparkling gold VIP pass. The red cord was pulled aside and we all walked in companionship to the bar.

"Compliments of the house . . ."

A bucket of ice and a bottle of champagne were placed before us at the bar. Popping the champagne, we all took a drink and adjusted to the surroundings.

"Wow, this really is VIP!"

As if electricity flowed through the air, connecting to all other bodies on the dance floor, I pumped a right fist into the air, shot pneumatically from the hips and shook to the rhythm of the drum and bass. Looking to Jade, I gave her a nod of acknowledgement, keeping to the rhythm of the bass I continued by turning my rhythm to face her. My right hand spurred her along as my left my left hand broke up aerospace to the underlying beat. Psi was just up ahead and he seemed to be in a level headed world of his own, cutting up shapes, grabbing the energy and tossing it in the air with the enthusiasm of an excited child. We owned the dance floor . . . Siobhan sidled over to us with an air of delight about her and Simon came jiving over like a jitterbug,

"Lucifer would like to make your acutance . . ."

As the bass was beginning to mix into another beat, Jade, Psi and I followed Siobhan from the dance floor to a grandeur stairwell that was guarded by another smartly dressed bouncer.

"Right this way,"

Coolly following Siobhan, I watched the other party goers with a joy in my heart. This was a real club experience that was filled with eager fresh-faced youths that were purely out to have a good time, and no trouble seemed to rear its ugly head. Everything in the club seemed luxurious, and this feeling continued to strike me as we made our way to the top of the stairwell. Softly clicking open the door, we entered into the ambient surroundings of what seemed to be a dragons den . . .

"Welcome," came the mans fluent and upbeat bass as it reverberated around the room, "Please come in, make yourselves comfortable . . ."

"Gabriel, Jade, this is my husband, Lucifer."

Even though the man was sat, an aura of prowess made this brawny and balding man a powerful presence. A welcoming smile played the features of his cleanly shaven face.

"I hear that you are head senator Gabriel . . ."

Stirring in the confines of an enveloping leather armchair, I thoughtfully received a goblet of wine that was brought round by a young woman in smart dress.

"Yes that's right Lucifer, I've been head senator for about 2 years now. You could say that I have the most powerful voice in the senate, but even this, as I'm sure your aware, has little avail . . ."

Lucifer nodded to the smartly dressed waitress as she left the room.

"Thank you Gabriel. Yes I am aware of how little avail you have achieved. This may sound blunt, but I know that it is not your fault as to why this is the case. How little power you have, I may say . . ."

"That's right, the government have complete control and they do what they want, unhindered. They create war for monetary gain, and keep people completely in the dark and therefore blind to what's truly going on!"

Lucifer and Gabriel had a fluency to their conversation that was a delight to watch . . .

"That's right, **Keeping** people in the dark. At the moment, a lot of people are more than *willing*, to naively sway with the mob. This form of World-wide rioting, makes it impossible for people to even realise, what Enlightenment is. We are *caught* in a web of disillusion, that has been put before us, by a Corrupt Government. To stop people from ever thinking for themselves Properly, the bullies of the world claim absolute power, and keep you in the Dark. This leads to a complete lack of understanding on our part, which apparently gives them the right, to turn people into slaves in a worldwide game of 'chess'."

It was truly refreshing to hear the truth about this fact of life.

"Very true Lucifer,"

"Egotistical, power hungry, war mongering, Elitist, Autocratic and Fascist 'individuals' who really control the world. Mass Enlightenment, and the toppling of this Fascist 'regime', is *the* struggle. Why do they have the right to be there? They're fucking the world up. Yet they still rule! They wish to keep they're 'earned' positions by any means 'necessary', and they don't care if they have to shit on the entire human race to do it."

Simon held his goblet of wine closely to his chest as he spoke,

"The egotistical, power that be, hold more information than what most of the populace are even aware of! Including the conspiracies surrounding UFO's. And that is unacceptable if we are ever to Evolve as a race. As with any Business, the bullies at the top are flexing they're tiny bit of dis/organised power, to the quivering work force at the bottom, us. It's about time we stood up to them . . . And have you ever noticed how all the people ever trying to do any good in this world are always Silenced . . . ? And the little Demons—who happen to be in power—are left to run amok?"

Lucifer rose from his seat and walked from the confines of his mahogany desk. Spinning a white board round in the wall,

"Now Gabriel, I have a little presentation for you if you would like to sit back for five minutes?"

The hostess proceeded to put a roll of film in a projector and Psi, Jade and Siobhan were just as enthralled and enthused as I was. I wondered what delight Lucifer had in mind . . .

"Now if there was a way to end our dependence on fossil fuels and create vast quantities of rain forest, would you give the notion a moment of recognition? It seems to have slipped through the net in the past, but now I am bringing it to light . . ."

The projector lit up the white board, and the heading simply read *Solar Lochs*, extending a metal pointer, Lucifer continued as the slide changed,

"Now all that has to be done is to create a dam that allows sea water to flow through a desalination plant via the force of gravity. Pure water can then be collected in concave concrete wells that are spread over a large area and are surrounded by a dome of glass or Perspex. This stops sand from filling the wells and amplifies the suns rays. When the lochs are filled, the resulting pure water will evaporate and an atmosphere of rain clouds will result. The Sahara desert and other areas of baron landscape will then turn into bountiful places where hemp and sugar cane may be grown. Sugar cane can then be processed into 100% alcohol for use in cars and this method is used in Mexico. It would stop our dependency on fossil fuels and create a clean burning fuel that is a lot cheaper than petrol." Lucifer chuckled to himself, "But don't mention that to the oil companies, as they wouldn't be too happy about it! This will ensure that rainforests are allowed to flourish and a clean burning fuel is allowed to be produced."

There are also plenty of jobs that will be created . . . Production of concrete and glass. Transportation and living areas for workers that could be sustained by the hydro electric produced by the dam. Saw mills for hemp and distillation plants for creating alcohol.

Summing up, Solar Lochs are specially designed lochs that collect and evaporate seawater. With this technology, an atmosphere of rain bearing clouds can be created in places such as the Sahara desert, South Africa and areas of South America, at all times of the year.

In Mexico, they use 100% alcohol to fuel their cars. Cheap, **clean** fuel that has infinite supplies. Sugar cane can be grown and then processed to create 100% alcohol that cars can be run on.

Villages may also flourish around the areas where clean water is produced. This may be an incentive to allow this project to go ahead . . . .

Lucifer compressed the pointer and clasped his hands before him.

"Now my empire was built from scratch. My father left me quite a fortune in his will and my first club was brought in 1993. I made sure that customers were treated first class, especially with the limo company. I now own 5 clubs, 12 limos and 1 casino. It is a very lucrative business I may say.

"Now my empire is nothing like the empires that tried to claim India. As soon as Britain withdrew from India the railway tracks used were rusted and ceased because the Indians had no training on how to use them. If we went in with education with proper schooling for everyone, the countries could fend for themselves, especially if a proper senate was in power and all the money could be shared evenly about the world . . . Fair trade."

Lucifer proceeded and sat down behind his desk,

"The people who support the National Guidance **Front** are blind and wish others to lead the same sad existence, of what they class as *life*. Completely blind and who are happy to do as they are told— even though most of them aren't aware that they are being guided Of course these rich people don't care for the poor of the world, even though—if they are smart enough—to know what this meant. Fuck that, I want a government that liberates the people to do as they want and live a life free from tyranny."

I nodded a silent acknowledgement,

"Now Gabriel, have you ever thought of how money could be saved and put to better uses for the community?"

"Well we have thought of a couple of things . . . How much Government officials get paid when we, the Senate work on minimum wage. And how much money is spent on sending *things* into space. Billions."

"Very good Gabriel. But have you ever thought of mentioning where all the money is and how it could be put to better uses? If there were a cap of say 250 million pound as a maximum in any one bank account, all those billions of pounds being hoarded by the bankers would be taken from them and spent on the people. It would sort not only our country out, to start with, but the entire world if they all took it onboard. If this was to take effect, corrupt governments would be out of power and the bankers wouldn't be the rulers of us all . . . Transporting funds, sums of money greater than 250 million to over sea accounts should be illegal . . ."

"Sounds very intriguing I must admit. Wouldn't you agree Gabriel?"

Psi allowed the thought time to imbue my mind.

"Very."

"I can see now your dogged determination Gabriel."

Lucifer interjected,

"Remember, I have the ability to keep the cameras rolling. When you gather enough support, summon me and I'll make sure of it . . ."

"I know what I must do . . ."

I looked to Jade and her aura of beauty, and I looked to Psi who nodded with warmth and friendship in his eyes.

"I wont let you down . . ."

Don't get too wrapped up in your everyday life, there is a bigger picture. This book has been written to open your eyes . . .

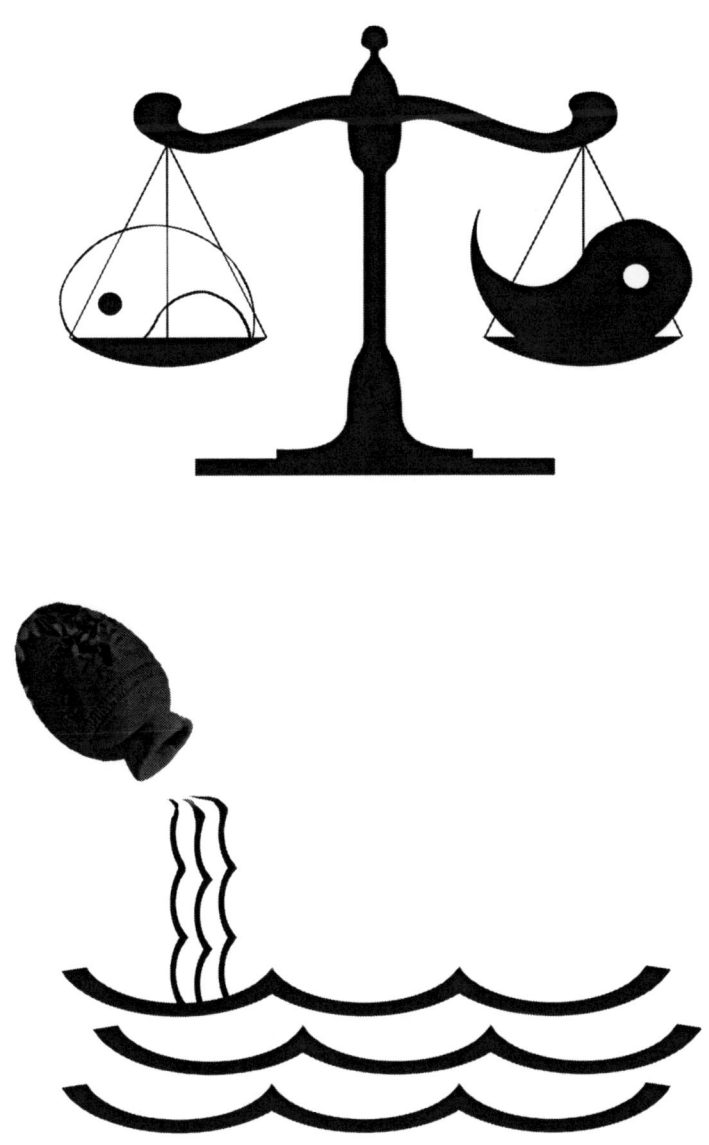

Flock To My Banner

BOOK 2
DREAMER

"I am the Psiphon filter, the medicine, the cure, and the water you drink, is what I have kept pure.

If you are unsure, take it from someone who knows the score. For those that are Naïve to true Loving law, how much do you expect one man to endure, as the one showing you the door."

The day had been a long affair, but not at all tedious. The clock on the wall read 9.30pm, and the final bustle of living loving maid employees, working at the new reduced minimum wage were flagging, but finally finishing for the night.

"Good night Mister, same time tomorrow!"

With a small pile of sheets to his right, he thought them small morsels of originality and fulfilling idiosyncrasies that would allow for an ever expanding consciousness, a peaceful night to ponder and dream free from the turmoil that seemed to take prescient in almost everyone's lives, even those that were aware . . .

"Yes goodnight Marcy, enjoy your night, what's left of it!"

"Will do. Heard Ricky gets it in the neck from B tonight, should be a goodn! How about yourself?

"Oh you know me Marcy" he said in a light hearted and joking tone, "Melodrama doesn't really appeal to me. I'm more concerned with the real thing!"

Marcy beamed with excitement as the thought of relaxing in front of the box had an infectious way of lightening the mood after a hard days work. The only thing that betrayed her beauty were the bags beneath her eyes.

"Ah your missing out, its reaching its crux, a couple more episodes than it really will hit the fan!"

With an always positive attitude, the man took the good points from all scenarios, even this had a slight satirical essence to it in his mind. When the shit hit's the fan . . . Never too lost in thought these days, only a moment went past before he replied.

"You enjoy Marcy," he said whilst tapping a pencil on the right side of his head. Thankfully however I still have a few papers to read over, some top quality ideas are taking shape inside these young adults minds you know!"

"Well this is the dawning of the age of Aquarius after all! Its about time we had some bright ideas, change this world for the better to take us out of this great depression!"

"Excellent Marcy. Glad your one of us. Shoulder to shoulder we stand in this life and the next! We're all in this together! And if one person steps out of line . . . One person is not important enough to spoil it for everyone else . . . even on a microscopic level."

The mans intellect knew everything of import, in accordance to having created inner peace. At the age of 27, his mind was still fresh and eager, and was as porous and ponderous as the day he reached high school and realised that an education, a true education, unhindered by anything including physical manifestations of the unresolved subconscious world, was very important.

He deduced that an educated mind can see things from many different angles and perspectives, especially in subjects that use the Right side of the brain including English and Art and Music. Even though in his younger days he was an adequate Mathematician, the whole certainty principle, could not be achieved, by the use of numbers.

He was also the type of man that only got hung up on things that affected a scenario or situation negatively, as it was normally the last thought on the thought path that resolved the issue, but of course, the work in progress was harangued every step of the way, until some form of logic could be created from being sucked into that disarraying black hole. Chaos . . . This mans tool was Plain English.

Taking aim, the man fired his empty cup of water with a flick at the bin 8 foot away. It bounced rim to rim before settling in a dark chasm amongst other anonymous trash, wondering how it found itself in such a vast and assorted array of garbage that would eventually be sorted by picking gulls and vultures . . .

"Good shot" Marcy piped. "Best one of the evening! I'm impressed!"

"Well sorting out the trash is kind of what I'm looking to do. Not to intentionally put you out of a job" he said with a chuckle. "The thing you next have to look forward to is me picking a fight with a half chewed honey dew melon rind."

Heading towards the door "So long as that's the only thing you knock the pulp out of Mr." she replied with comical wit. "Also, we don't want to see your handsome face bruised now do we. Melon rind vs. bean pole, what are the odds?"

With a smile, "quite likely, aaand 50-50 I would say. Don't take the pith now, that would just add insult to injury as I bathe my hands in tcp."

"TLC?" Marcy chided as if she accidentally misheard him. Always willing to see the brighter side to life. "Enough of that, any garden would flourish!"

With a chuckle at her light heartedness, "complete understanding. Very thoughtful Marcy . . ."

As the door clicked shut, the man thoughtfully watched his female colleague distance herself down the hallway until she turned a corner and was finally out of sight. Soon to be away from a place that consumed so much of her time. A thankless, boring and monotonous task, day in, day out, to barely make ends meet, in a life of *westernised* miserable *luxury* and virtual poverty. Times were hard, and quality of life was degrading by the minute in one big bubbling cooking pot, she unfortunately had to face every evening.

The man was just doing his bit to help a troubled schizophrenic back on track by sharing time in a light hearted, but none the less, Loving way. Deep down the man new she was dealing with issues that were either passed down a generation, or fobbed off by those who were still closed minded and looked to judge as they thought they were better than everyone else. Leaving the issues for someone else to deal with, and then ultimately label, tread on, dismiss, persecute and look down their nose at the ones doing them the biggest favour their wis.

But low and behold, the man had one the race. Realisation with no funky shit. He knew, that mental illness was torture . . . No one was there for him, everyone was against him. That's why he's there for everyone else, he wouldn't wish it on anyone. He keeps you from the worst, and shows you the light . . .

Traipsing through the pristine hallways pondering many things that those from Venus ponder, including lustrous fantasies with an ideal partner, as well as ways to remove spanners of anger and unresolved issues from the works to finally get a moments peace . . . amongst all of these things, a flier caught the corner of Marcy's eye as she slowed past the vast array of different notices on the 20 foot wide cork notice board. It read;

"**Horse meat Scandal**, so how long were they misleading customers for? I think it's time some of these businesses paid out some hard earned cash in compensation for being the slightest misleading as the ingredients read **Beef.** But of course, the issue just got swept under the carpet, is that a challenge to Find us. And as a matter of principle?!"

The euphemism brought around a studious hatred as things of such a matter still happened in our modern day in age. Just imagine what Ethiopians eat! Oh yeah,—nothing . . .

Further along the board, it was as if this particular flier was radioactive as the area surrounding it was clear of any bureaucracy or *misleading propaganda*. The *latter* was part of a master plan, who knows how people set these things up . . .

Automatons no shun the evil ways

Parioujhanoia, how open minded are ya, was it before or was it after, that you suffered your disaster?

No longer blind you struggle to find, down a dark path that binds. Exorcising demons as you try to create, some peace of mind.

So with no one to hold your hand, Pandora's box is open your mind therefore the substance has been banned, by a hierarchy who have slaveries plan, surely this cant all come undone by the power of one man.

So my energy's free, might just set you free, jump up and down with glee, as we all just simply be.

So as I reach the Gate, after a Perfect day when I wake, adhering to my Fate, as I feel in Heavenly state.

So sit back and smile, for those that are free and have smashed the last mile,

We have been betrayed this last while by those who seek to judge and keep us all on file.

So don't come crying to me, when they dash all your hopes and dreams, make it clear for all to see, that there is such a thing, as a Peaceful reality, whilst sowing seeds of Loving Totality.

Hendrix Cares for no body—

Even before the core of the poem was given time to imbue the mind, Marcy stood with a gaping jaw. Not so much because of the wordage of the poem she had just read on the communal notice board,

Aching Heart of a Schizophrenic that have they're moments;

"What's that bit that's blanked out? All it says is Hendrix cares for no body . . ."

Somewhere in this fragile woman ached with grief beyond relief. Cant see the forest for the trees.

HOME

"C'mon . . . c, ah success"

The key fit perfectly, worked its magic—and the sturdy door with dents from previous attempts, swung wide. A slight smell of old mildew from being a Victorian building with no direct sunlight was the familiar scent that welcomed me back to what was now my humble, but none the less tidy and roomy abode.

When the three of us were in, I checked how much leckie was in the meter, satisfied that it would last at least another night, I closed the door and locked it. The usual drill when I got home, to forget the world outside.

"As you know guys, I don't trust any fucker."

Acclimatising to our cool surroundings on a fine summers evening, Will placed his 24 crate with enthusiasm on the kitchen counter which overlooked the sitting and dining area. Clicking fingers from outstretched arms, he proceeded to open the box like an expert that had had plenty of practice.

Chucking a beer to Matthew, the veteran caught it in one hand and cracked it in an instant without so much as a glimpse.

"Woohooo . . . lets get this party started!"

Looking to me, he offered by a gesture of a mid height swoosh from the hips, a solid finger homing in on its alcoholic target.

"Ah you know I'm not touchin any of that pish water tonight man"

"Not even the one t whet yer whistle?"

"Weird heads man, cant risk it . . . I can smoke and smoke and smoke until the cows head back to their fields, but drink, ah its torture. Demon drink for me man!"

"Normally it's the other way round" chirped Matthew. "Most people get paranoid on pot rather than drink, unlucky for you that your preference happens to break the law."

"I know aye. I much prefer smoke by another league anyway."

Matty also liked to dabble, lucky for him, neither smoke nor drink affected him adversely. He continued with invisible wit that was masked with seriousness.

"Don't you feel bad for breaking the law?"

Matty had to try his hardest to keep a straight face and from bursting out with laughter.

However, I knew Matthew from a very young age. He also knew me, but I thought I would let him believe he got me by continuing in a pissed off manner,

"Fuck the law and system that's in place now. People who need to be governed. In other words told what to do. We are the law, because we stick to the rules of self control and equality"

"Ha ha, I was only joking lol. Getting yourself all hot and bothered."

"Ha ha you're a cheeky bastard. We are the law because we show people the Loving way."

Joining Matthew on the couch opposite him, will took a seat next to him. Remotely turning on the high fi, I proceeded to roll a joint of the best and oiliest pollie going . . . ;

I think the album had something to do with bells and there being a divide. They will never know, but do ya think, maybe there is a way that they will know . . .

Cracking open a tin of energy juice, brute, I guzzled like a hummingbird drinking nectar. I'm sure that even if I tried I wouldn't be able to get my wings to move as fast as that fuckers. Well, you gotta be good at something in life. (I don't really watch tv).

Relaxing back in the enveloping couch, Will piped in his bedruggled but none the less wide awake state. Taking a large swig of beer,

"Aye people being governed, look at how well those in power in Egypt and Argentina were lowering the standard of life for your common man and severely pissing them off in the process . . ."

Matt interjected after a moment of wist,

"That's it, at least these people had the initiative to kick out their hierarchy by peacefully demonstrating. I mean how can that many people be wrong. Even with that many people against him, Egypt's president still tried his best to cling onto that power. The military eventually had to step in to get him out. After a time though, Egypt's old president still got his loyal henchmen police officers to kill 600 innocent civilians!"

Matt continued as he looked thoughtfully to the middle distance,

Our western world is corrupt as anything in Limbo, its just hidden beneath a vale, and the true reality lurks just beneath the surface like a snake. The rich get richer and more 'powerful', whilst of course the workforce who make up the majority of our populace are forever being made poorer, and less empowered by mps (and secret 'powers') who give themselves pay rises and illegally tax your ass. Just as well you only have 1 bedroom cuz!

Its like the power will have to be prized from their live rhigomortist hands with a crowbar"

Extinguishing the joint, my mind was bombarded by the kicking bass of track 2 and was highly stimulated by rousing talk. My senses were blasted to overdrive. The convection current of smoke danced around on the airways like notes on a classic sheet that cascaded, expanded and engulfed the mentality in a very spiritual manna. A heightened sense of self . . .

"Spot on Matt. These are tender times. And as it stands, its a house of cards . . . The western world needs to rise by peacefully protesting to get rid of our fascist hierarchy. It has to be peaceful protests as we don't want Martial law. It is people like us who open the eyes of others as to what's truly going on and blow this travesty away as it is the antithesis of what is good.

If you don't believe me, then how come world peace hasn't been created yet. Every hierarchy there is at this moment in time will quite happily watch you suffer, as they just take, bully, terrorise, murder and own you. They're like a poisonous cancer. And you support your owners every step of the way as you try and cast people like me out, the one helping you with real life and its qualities, life is hard, but with having no one breathing down your neck! There needs to be a voice of the people . . . Suggestion boxes.

Don't tell me its going to become an *iron*ised house of cards. That isn't so easy to blow down if its welded together by evil . . . there would be all out war in the universe . . . we are already on Mars . . ."

With intellect, Matthew interjected after a brief silence of words, with some communal knowledge to brush up on some points, as he also had a very cleverly analytical brain to add to some points,

"All out war in the universe eh? So were not alone then. Weapons for all occasions. I can see why it's a tender couple of years, as it will either take off and accelerate to new heights with a true Democratic and Peaceful Senate in place,—am I right so far cuz?—or it will crash and burn and there would be an eternity of Darkness. Who knows what states of consciousness could be reached with anti-matter weapons, obey or you will be destroyed. Annihilation. That's what happens if you support our current hierarchy, and ultimately the Evil One paedophile . . . And you wonder why technology is the devils work. Don't let the Devil in, let almighty God into your hearts . . ."

Rapping the backs of my fingers and knuckles on my jeans,

"Iv got a pleasant surprise . . ."

I reached into my pocket, opened my wallet and picked out a 40 pound wrap of speed I got from our top quality contact earlier in the day. (in secret of course). All of our eyes immediately lit up with barely contained excitement!

"Still a class B chaps, so were not breaking any more laws compared to the smoking of the gange . . . A persons free choice to do what they want to do eh, what the hell is wrong with that?!

And of course you have all been duped naïve as you drink your drug and judge and condemn those who choose to do other drugs, you bunch of hypocrites. There are better drugs out there than alcohol!"

I was becoming quite a connoisseur when it came to spin. Now there was dynamite, then there was stuff that was in a league of its own. Producing my fraud star bank card, I opened the foil wrap and chopped off 3 healthy half gram portions of the most potent space base paste that would wire the three of us to the moon . . .

We all sat as if huddled around the psychedelically coloured motif that lay on the floor between the two sofas,

"After three. One, two, three,"

We placed our amusement for the night on the tip of our tongues, and sucked it like a sweetie,

"Yah that is the good shit . . ." The most stinging sensation of chemical burn to the tongue and roof of the mouth . . .

"Yah yah, dat isht goot yah. Voondabah!"

Knowing the score from having done this many times in the past, with varying quality until a solid reliable contact was found, I knew that we would feel something for the first 45 minutes, then that feeling would reach its apex, and then we would shoot off into space where there wasn't a dull moment for a good 10 or 11 hours . . . most excellent. This stuff was the best yet . . .

"To answer your rhetoric Matt, correct, we aren't alone in the universe, and they aren't just Grey . . ."

Being one of the cleverest beings in existence, I cast my photographic memory over different,

Ooh I'm starting to feel something, that familiar feeling of progressing euphoria and empowerment

Things that related to this topic of race.

"If you cant take a human for who they are and you are still getting hung up on the colour of another humans skin, how are you supposed to get on with those that aren't human? Of course this misguided hatred and anger is just a physical manifestation of unresolved past and bad teaching that leads to people lashing out, and of course through this, separation as everyone is *riddled* with reciprocated enmity. It's the mind that makes a person and not the clothes that they wear."

Matthew asked in a curious tone,

"So if they're not just Grey, what other races are there?"

I also knew everything of import, but there were still some things that I didn't know. Some things were just left to speculation and estimates. Including race hierarchy, and how they're systems operated. We are still very young as a race. **Rise**.

"Well other than Greys, (the Lord looking down on us from the 'stars') there are Lizard People, Symbiots, Scuttlers Insectoids and biomasses . . .

Can you see now that these next 2 years are very tender, I need to stick around and help you through it. Your supposed to protect me! We need technologies sword to rest in the hands of a Peaceful Human Race. Other than the travesty that has become this modern day and age."

"How you guys feelin?" I continued.

The smiles on their faces already told the story.

"Pretty fuckin good!"

"Aye, excellent. Absolutely brilliant."

"Good stuff eh, still got plenty left. We have yet to peak! Ill roll another spliph . . ."

With an endless stream of garbage . . .—curse the place.

Soliloquy of a lost Soul

Numbed feign in his late teenage years, when magic no longer filled the air—used up by those who took it for granted, without giving anything back. In its place stood an insurmountable monolith of despair, as dark as any thought that he tried his hardest to keep reeled back, every waking moment, of every day. And when they escaped, it seemed to him that anyone close to him, could see his every thought. After time he realised that this *is* what they gave back.

How long do you think it was before he came to this realisation . . . ?

. . .   my

. . .   heads

. . .   fucked

Obviously not soon enough, as the damage had already been done. There was no going back. It would take many years to cure the poison that flowed through his brain, but of course, this nameless curse, from me to you—**no end** in *sight*.

Where would you have started he asks in rhetoric.

Mid point was sorting through the shambles that had been his entire life. Little snippets of movie reel to keep you all amused, and at times disgusted, as you feel it within yourself to have the power to outcast an outcast, and judge whilst he slowly died inside. At the same time not only having to keep every being in existence happy, but sort everything out in a way that was as easy as possible to understand, as even one thought was enough to hinder a work in progress. He laughed at this euphemism. This was before he realised that he wasn't the only one with a brain capable of thought. At the time he was defenceless . . .

Part of the sub-conscious, coming through in waking life. As time went on, he couldn't ask for more of an audience. And in his adult years, the persecution for being the one that spoke, broke him once again. 24 onwards, he shone and realised that he *eventually* spoke by choice, and was not coaxed into it by even a single thought that existed, even for the shortest of times possible; as far as Universal thought goes he talked the undisputed truth, but he had to ask, was this a delusion beyond belief?

As he hadn't said 2 words, he said one. Reflect

FORESIGHT

"It was good to see that Gabriel had done his bit, if it wasn't for his hard work and courage over the past two years, we really would have been up shit creek."

Psi let his hands fall from the metal bars that held him prisoner.

"Do you miss him?"

Turning to face J, a young man in his 20s who was his cell mate for the next few months for growing cannabis plants,

"Like no other. He was a brother."

Psi continued in a light hearted manner,

"He is however, elsewhere, doing his bit for the benefit of us all . . ."

"He became a household name! I used to watch him make mincemeat of the NGF at the senate arena. Opening the eyes of all who chose Love over the *seemingly* easier option of greed that puts the world to shit."

"Yes he was very good at that, his wife Jade empowered and fueled him. She is another innocent that has had to suffer Love and loss. You push anyone in a corner enough, they will lash out. Gabriel did this for liberation of the people. Liberation for people such as yourself, young J. Growing a natural plant, glad your not in for anything else."

J continued as the young man realised that it was people that were important, he was becoming a good friend of Simons. They looked out for each other.

"Aye a fuckin plant eh! What these artards have to realise is that all chemicals are fundamentally natural. They can all be found on the periodic table!

"Ah the whole drug thing" Psi rocked in his chair, cocked his head back and chuckled. "Gabe really drilled that one across a couple of years ago, so much so that the current political climate is now 35-65 National Guidance **Front**. I wonder what will spark the next political shift . . ."

"Well its 6.50 Psi. Soon be time for our daily dose of a 35% reality check. They're really beginning to crack down. I wonder what stupidity these naughty beasts will spew up next . . ."

"I'll swap you 3 fags for your last diazepam brother?"

"Oooh you drive a hard bargain Psi, how did you know I just finished my last one?"

"Great powers of deduction chap. Plus my x-ray vision helps a bit."

"That's funny man. And there was me thinking its cos I lived in a glass cell."

Even though there was always an atmosphere, it didn't enter this particular cell or mingle with its occupants. Producing the vallie, Psi handed over three cigarettes. Inspecting the small blue tablet, he proceeded to neck it without any water, then he went all the way to the other side of the cell and flicked on the tube.

"This buds for you . . ."

"A couple of pints of that legal drug alcohol would go down a treat just now. Get high and all touked oup causy with the saups."

J was famous for bursting out with things at certain times. It was like comical tourrettes.

"Brute. Feel your muscles expand as you pound down this killer mix of secret ingredients,"

Psi proceeded to read out the small print on the bottom of the screen,

"May cause sudden and unexplained death."

"Almost as bad as those bloody anti psychotics then" Psi concluded.

"Quiet please"

The oval council chamber hushed,

"Gentleman speaker, please initiate"

There was no beating around the bush any more. This cut throat business was straight to the point. It was a battleground where the NGF had maintained a hold over the verges of no mans land.

As it was on senate grounds, they were always allowed to begin the debate.

"Sources leaked that cigarettes and alcohol may soon become illegal. We are wondering how this would be possible from all the revenue that is generated from tax on these substances, as well as a persons free choice to do what they want to do." ka maroon stood at his podium, his watery eyes and pale clammy face pretty much summed up what this party were all about. Jellyfish and snakes.

"You know we don't reveal plans in their early stages. You know we enforce law as and when we have fully fledged ideas and when we see fit, for the benefit of the people . . .

Other than the obvious, the senators were struck dumb, as they new that it would just lead to the same thing. Going round in circles, *chasing tail of a dogma.* None of them were as quick or as good at analysing as Gabriel. The Senate wasn't the same without him as they're leader. He would have seen in an instant and brought it immediately to light with what would seem obvious to him and was obvious to Psi.

Psi enlightened an on the edge of his seat J. otherwise he would have been disappointed, as it meant another stroke to the bastard NGF. Which unfortunately was to be the case with this particular congregation.

"Well all this money they're gonna make off of they're dodgy dealings with the Saudi hierarchy, they wont need money from taxation of cigarettes and alcohol. Deliberately dumbing down the nation to believe that the government knows what is best for them. They want complete control, and they want your lives to be as miserable as possible. ka maroon struck a pose, but looked even more of a stupid idiot than he did a moment before.

"We'll sort it out with a little wager then. Keystone college Oxford. A new college of Enlightenment. They're a very mixed bunch. What with one of the laws, what was it again, he said looking down his nose, *equality?* Depending on the outcome of this college alone, the next student election, will determine which party rules over all college and university political dealings in the whole of Britain . . . dare you wager . . .

Counselling;

1 year in, still had 5 years left. Psi felt his anger bubbling like a pit of tar. Defending an innocent man. A Brother. Hired assassins get away with murder, I get done with attempted murder. No way,

I don't think of regret, like I say, I was defending a Brother. Apart from the regret of not having a fucking uzi . . .

Still careening about the injustice that cost his best friend his life, day after day, minute after minute, ate away at every fibre of Psi's being, and with no end in sight, he could see things taking a turn for the worst. *Who was doing the counselling.* He realised that he must embrace his anger so that it didn't control him. It burned to his core. He began to centre his emotions and let go of all those manifestations which were linked to that toxic dead weight of burden. Now centred, true emotion shot off into space. Gabriel would have it no other way. For he wanted what was best for everyone.

Soliloquy of a lost Soul, reprise

Can anybody hear me, he uttered in turmoiled rhetoric both mentally and physically on his most tortuous day to date. Cos I can hear you, or at least I think I can, the true you, that doesn't have a good word to say. At a stage 4/6th of the way through, who was there to tell him the unspoken language lov—was real, or not real.

How many people did he expect to answer that question, how was he supposed to distinguish between or be at peace with the constant bombardment of terrible morphing picture and language that assaulted his mind and made him sick to his stomach. The blackest Chaos possible. Terminal ambiguity that ate away at his heart. There was still yet about 400 more of these sessions to endure, 6 hours each time. So with time, the remedy, the **cure.** Do you really think it not possible for him to point out any look, from an invisible being, without even looking at them?

This is the start of the stopping of looking. The most clear, precise, compact, logical, truthful and undeniable compensateries and idioms for every working mind, that was starting to work out of its apathy.

Knowing only too well that either no one could hear him, or everyone could, was a paradox of unequalled proportion, but who could he ask? No-one was giving an angstrom, instead, they were taking a yard, he was the one walking a thousand miles into the wilderness.

Being the guide, Everyone's footsteps were now falling perfectly into place, with everything in sync, people **finally** *reflecting*, only 5 years later than when he first of all told them to do so. All issues were in their appropriate place, and were finally being dealt with and resolved. Reflection on planet Earth, where no-one sees it . . .

The looking finally stopped. **You**—can reflect in peace.

Did you have to queue up for your poetic licence . . .

Clearing the air of that rotten putridicity, he still found however, that a lot of folk changed like the limp wind.

He carried on carving a bloody path, regardless whether they could hear him or not, he had come too far, it was his job. That is why his spirit, and mind, ruled by his heart, wrote so easy. Some people seemed to think him stupid. As it was normally the final thought on the thought path that resolved the issue and created complete clarity. Of course, impatience is a vice, as you continued to support evil if their was even an instant, of something that seemed anything but perfect.

The English was so plain that it stood out, and the message was very clear . . .

Every *being* in existence.

Anger (and all of its manifestations), Schizophrenia, bi-polar, manic depression, lack of understanding, and unresolved sub conscious issues had all been cured.

All who have **Stopped** *sinning* were welcome on the safe side of his Impenetrable Wall of Pure White, Soul Light.

SPEED KING

With 2 and a half grams of speed left, I placed it in the usual fibred pocket of my wallet which was ripe with the smell of constantly breaking the law. Standing to attention, as if rising to an unspoken purpose, I slid my wallet skilfully and elegantly into my pocket.

"So were meeting Marcy and co. in half an hour then chaps."

Matthew and Will acknowledged me by ching chinging the air with their 6th tin,

"Going down like water boss."

Solid as a rock and malleable as red hot iron, the nuclear rod which was my constant was again ignited and the flames burned bright. I fell back into the couch, with outstretched left leg and a right hand that followed through the air as the energy in my fist landed perfectly on my invisible target in accordance to my centre of balance.

I had definitely peaked

"Shit hot eh!!"

"Oh aye. Definitely the best stuff so far!"

The euphoria album which sounded fuller than usual with its peaking trills, rat a tats, soothing vocals and electronic bass sounded tender as it harmonised with our extremely heightened senses. This wasn't trippy speed, it was ten times better.

"Build a joint then Matt."

"Pass over your politics then cuz."

With roughly 5 and a half grams of pot remaining, I gathered up the baccy, skins and roach and passed the healthy looking lump over. Don't be fooled. Every waking moment whilst feeling this high was a working art form . . .

Will suddenly produced his phone and held it in front of him without even the thought of micro shakes, as the people you cant see weren't putting things out of sync by polluting the airways with their unresolved shit that they took out on others. Because they were also high.

"Take a look at some of these pictures man, they're good."

"Ah Will ya pervert. What delights you got in store for us?"

"What made you think its porn?"

"Well I have known you for over 6 years now!"

"Alright. You got me. Its porn."

Matthew chuckled as he began to stick the papers together,

"Would it be anything else? Me thinks not likely."

Will started up the slide show with two second intervals,

"Bloody hell man, where did you get these from?! Ooh that's a goodn!"

Will chuckled to himself in a self satisfied manner,

"aand that one. Goggle images of course, just turned the filter off, wouldn't surprise me if I go blind sometime soon man."

"Don't be silly. You'll just get hair sprouting out of the palms of your hands. At least you went to spectators so your vision should be just fine I'm sure."

Sprinkling the last crumble into the joint, Matt took a look with a craned neck,

"Its surprising what you can get on the internet these days, anything you want just a few keys and clicks away . . ."

Filling the joint with tobacco, he rolled finger and thumb, and then again, licked the gum, and stuck the delightfully filled skins around the pay load. Another perfectly rolled joint!

Putting in the roach, he sparked it up, held the joint between fore and middle finger and toked. Blowing out a plume, he continued to hold his hands in front of him in a raised and solid stationary stance, as he looked at Will's phone just by moving his eyes.

Some of the stances we pull off. No wonder doctors read body language, snakes that they are. Except they're not that glamorous or intelligent.

"Aye and one day it will be the ruler of us all if those that lurk just beneath the surface get into power. Any music or videos that you own that aren't copyrighted, would mean a jail sentence. And how would they check this, I wonder," Will mused.

"I'v got one story as far as the internet goes and how curiosity killed the cat—she just had to go back to it. She saved the day, but such a monumental moment can only last so long.

It was like a metal ball falling down a tiered pinball machine to its escape at the bottom. Half way through the metal balls journey,

'Stop there moo, they'll build up your hopes again and just laugh at you as they dash them.' They played a game that suckered in. The internet is evil,

'Something scared ya,'

I saw this without seeing it. I'm that perceptive.

'I think I just saved the day' as she slid across the bolt at the bottom of the enigma machine that prevented the ball from escaping. What's changed . . . ?"

Hospital Daze

"Well procycladine helps with side effects of medication & when I suffer anxiety."

Looking to the middle distance

. . .

Looking sharply at the doctor,

"Don't worry, I'm not hallucinating."

After a moment & deliberation,

"Well surely the thought of there being something there or not is a form of hallucination?" The doctor remarked in deep cocky-serious & derogatory tone. My how he was a master of his craft.

"Well surely if you perceive what I see then surely you must be a schizophrenic."

The doctor involuntarily jerked in air and shrewd away from the brain. The meeting was brought to a close.

Listening through the door,

"No more procycladine, lets see how he fairs up a few weeks of withdrawal and therefore side effects.

The shaking got worse & worse.

"I'm sure that balding bastard is laughing while he hangs upside down to sleep."

"Aye, whos that . . ."

"You are taking this medication even if we have to pin you down and inject you against your will.

"What about my baby!?!

"Well you should have thought about that before you got mental illness." The doctor said in a deep cocky-serious and derogatory tone."

"How can you?!!"

"Because in here, and soon to be welcomed into all your homes, I'm God."

Yes these anti psychotics are not only horrid to take for side effects, they may cause damage to unborn children & may cause sudden & unexplained death. They're talking about all of you, not just those currently in hospital, even those in the community. Yes, the community, & how you must bow down to doctor Owen.

"Who d'ya think . . . ?" the man asked in rhetoric

"One of Robert Sons reprobates,"

"Ah, the beast . . ."

"Aye. On another note however, did you hear about Glack-so building they're new chemical making plant? 25 million spent to create "respiratory medication.""

The other man chortled as if he new what was coming.

"Aye that'll be right. More like for the production of more anti psychotics. All they want to do is dope up the nation and welcome them to the community lol.

"Not really a laughing matter though. All done in secret now with everyones blind acceptance remember!".

"Aye"

"You remember Finlay"

Tick, tick, 4 minutes of the usual mundane had been made bearable.

"Oh aye, the kiddie from Skye?"

"Aye. Ended up in Karstairs.

"Aye, what the criminally insane hospital?"

"Aye. Gave some prick of a doctor 2 black eyes as he was deliberately riling him up."

"That seems a bit of a harsh penalty for something so minor."

"Aye your telling me, I can only imagine the horror stories of that place. This place is bad enough. How I can only wonder how bad it must be for him. He's a good man. Sorry bro.

"Lets break him out," the man said half heartedly

"He shouldn't fuckin be there. Bastard Doctors!!!

As the man shouted the final point with rage . . .

KISSING GATE

I continued,

"Sleep paralysis . . ."

Matthew outstretched his joint hand to meet me half way after taking his 6th toke. Excited to be handed one of my favourite drugs,

"Cheers Matt." adopting a similar stance, I took a hefty toke. Enjoying the moment, I collected my thoughts . . .

"Aye—sleep paralysis. Never have you felt more tired, or heavy, in a state of half sleeping lucidity using every last bit of effort to prop yourself at an angle, as something not human creeps from the shadows and into the room."

"Will and Matthews ears pricked."

"I had to bite a chunk out of an Alien one night as it tried to break my ribs—then I woke.

The eerie schizoid melody was the only reality that filled the air at that moment.

On a lighter note however, a gangly limbed Grey gave me sleep paralysis one night. It snapped off after great effort and I strangled him half to death. I let him go when I thought he had had enough after I nearly snapped its neck, and low and behold he was friendly!

I apologised for strangling him, and he told me his name was Marasque. We are not alone.

Taking another toke as I relaxed back into the sofa,

It happened to be on the night I saw a ufo go nose to nose with a plane and weave around the outside of it. Just before heading to bed, I was star gazing and I saw a bit *plink* off of a star, as it continued on a downward journey, eventually being blocked out of view by buildings on the horizon level. It's strange because things just seemed to work out so perfectly. It was a very weird night. And as I woke, 4 o clock, the dead of morning, I realised I was not alone. There was a throaty clicking on the roof . . ."

The song ended. Silence.

. . .

"Man you know how to give the spooks! Remarked Will as he swallowed the lump in his throat,

Far from tired as the time neared 10.50, it was hard to imagine the state that was just described.

Shaking off the eerie bound feeling, Will continued the conversation in a confident manner,

"Analysing the sky one night I saw two ufo's crossing paths, and even seen stars spinning on their axis. That is however about as Paranormal as I have experienced,"

Slowly kicking out my right leg, I proceeded to lean forward and outstretch my right arm with joint in hand which Will skilfully intercepted between fore and middle finger. Briefly raising his right hand as a gesture of thanks, he pursed his lips around the final third of the joint and toked as Matthew piped up.

"That's another reason why this sort of thing is illegal man, the government don't want us opening our minds!"

I interjected,

"Very true. They don't like this kind of talk as this sedition will set people free."

—

"With the right drugs we could fly out of that door any minute,"

"Well that's just about were what to do. Come on guys get your shit together. We've got to meet Marcy at the kissing gate in 10 minutes."

The sturdy oak door banged shut behind us as we breathed in the cool summer night air,

"What a glorious evening, it has been a great summer so far. Best in a few years!"

Clicking heels of designer trainers on the cobbled backstreet in smart jeans an t-shirt, we also looked good with eyes that beamed and tracked the females in an interested and respectful manner. Out of earshot,

"Check that out man, women come in her size?!"

Sharing in a chuckle, we headed on to our destination.

"So what sort of drugs we talking about bro?" Matthew asked Will in an intrigued tone.

Will took a brief inhalation of summer air before continuing,

"Oooh serious ones that literally would allow you to fly if you explored enough and gained enough knowledge."

Pausing briefly,

"Don't worry, we're not talking heroin here"

"Nah fuck that man" I interjected with vehemence.

Will continued in a wise and sympathetic manner as Matthew listened intently,

"DMT brothers . . . a complete view of the universe. Don't do too much though, or you will just end up in a hole, but I'm telling it would blow your mind. Low and behold it will soon be made illegal."

In a state that didn't leave us longing for the next high, we continued in companionship as the kissing gate came into view.

"This particular drug stimulates the pineal gland of the brain, what is made up of the same material as your eyeball. Just think of all the limitless possibilities that can be achieved as the different viewing lenses of your Third Eye are brought to focus on anything you want imaginable and tangible. This is also the case when you dream."

"Sounds good" me and Matthew said a second apart.

"That's not all folks"

Now an interest in the topic really was beginning to be kindled, Will continued,

"The crashed ufo's found by the Germans had a similar receptor in place, to the pineal gland. They reverse engineered the *chair* which housed such a receptor, and it could be used by trained scientists to travel anywhere, any time in the universe that they wish to. But past the 23rd of December 2012, this remains a mystery . . . This requires people evolving from the Dark Age . . . If people don't rise to the cause of almighty God, Planet Earth will turn into a place which turns its inhabitants into a race of soldiers, rather than a bountiful world where Angels rule . . . There is no greater honour than becoming an Angel. As you earn your Wings . . ."

The *swansong* of such a speech rang perfectly clear.

"Nice one Will."

Paying the three pound admission, I was the first to enter the club and I immediately let my Wings shoot out from my back. Perfect balance for a special occasion. The dance floor however would have to wait a while before I graced it with the Pegasus tattoo on my ankle. Pegasus being the large northern constellation near Aquarius.

Closely followed by my 2 favourite comrades, we made our way to the bar, and as the man with cash,

"What you lads drinking?"

Will licked his lips in a comical way as if slavering uncontrollably for his next drink,

"Uuum, I think ill go for a blueberry cider!"

In a similar way Matthew drooled over the taps of different guest pints.

"Ill go for a toffee apple cider cuz."

"And a tin of brute please."

Turning from the bar, the three of us spectated the dance floor as only a couple of semi pros were whetting the grind stone of the drum and bass.

Drinks in hand we surveyed the bustle and clocked Marcy. She wasn't alone. Not intimated however, quite the opposite as it looked like a large group of young ladies, we sleuthed like the cool cats we were to the corner of the club.

Immediately rising from her seat, Marcy shouted with glee as she rolled her hands towards herself as if to speed up our progress.

"Hello guys, Great to see ya come on take a seat!"

Marcy excitedly patted the long leather couch that was surrounded by tables and occupied chairs.

The introductions were made. These 4 women—not including Marcy—ranged from the ages of 19 to 28 and were all beautiful, as well as in some form of higher education. Honeypot.

A seductive glance was thrown my way from 2nd furthest away table as the hushed voices of the two ladies was drowned out by the Skrilling dub step.

Matthew also clocked the look, after a couple of seconds he jibed,

"Does she ring your bell?"

With a chuckle

"Oh aye. The two of em."

Closing my left eye in the least possible way in their direction pretending I didn't notice, they also pretended not to notice.

As the night progressed, we began to mingle. Matthew was sitting talking with Marcy and his new friends Sarah and Julie. Sparks were beginning to kindle.

Will was flirting freely with Heather.

Whilst I was talking with the Beauty of the group, Madeleine . . .

"So what do you like?" She asked in a genuine and bordering on seductive tone,

"Oh I like lots of things . . . Including sex. I said in the bluntest and most comical sense possible. Hoping she would pick up on the humour and not leave me hanging,

"Well that's a dead cert, play your cards right you can have me all night!"

Feeling an exothermic reaction, I rejoiced with glee inside as the 5th notch on the bed post would soon be hit on the spot.

"Yess" I celebrated fondly. She didn't mind. If anything she was also rejoicing.

"So what do you like."

After a moments thought

"Uuumm, sex. Lots of things really. Anything that's original and has some thought to it . . ."

Intrigued, in the utmost way as in the company of beautiful women,

"What don't you like?"

"Hmmm. Those that break the law and don't adhere to Love."

"So your in full time education then Madeleine?"

The 26 year old led to everything except a dull moment.

"Yeah this is my second year studying maths at keystone college. Ooohh it's a challenge. It will soon be the student elections. And I know who im voting for . . .

Another thing I don't like is paying taxes on my 16 hour a week wage at pirate island . . ."

"Ah taxes, one other thing we have all experienced. That ones the renegade. Did you know there is no law in place that states you must pay them on your working wage? Its just the hierarchy's—our owners—way of making themselves richer and us poorer. Quickly now before they make it law, (at Christmas when all these things are changed in secret) just think of how much you would make from a tax rebate!"

"Ooohh I like a man that knows his stuff. A Real turn on!"

"So who you gonna vote for in the upcoming student elections?"

"Well it sure wont be the Enlightenment party, I heard a rumour that its founder once showed his heart to death, with dire consequences. No way am I voting for a man that dances with death . . ."

"But hes a good man he wants whats right!"

"And the spritual death of 4 children is right? Not a fuckin chance, im voting NGF."

The ladies overheard the change in tone and tempo and immediately remarked, so am I, me too, and me.

"Yes but almighty God is all powerful. He'll be able to heal that."

"Yes. But I also heard that he was immaculate with some women,"

"Who did you hear all these *rumours* off?"

"Marcy . . ."

The night had taken a sudden nose dive . . .

A lost soul briefly passed through the room to try its best in a hopeful manner to help complete clarity: Marcy picked out slight imperfections that really did her head in because she liked him so much. Even the slightest thing—the end of the poem about the man she loved—sent her into psychosis and she talked her friends into voting otherwise.

Soliloquy of a Lost Soul, Finally at Peace . . .

So would you really think anything else would be the case as he had a look at the airways from a 3 dimensional perspective heightened sense. Where a 2 dimensional mentality was the norm?

He realised that the majority of the populace, were descendants of slaves. Not much had changed, and not much had been done to quell the misguided condemnation that was bought about by spoon fed siphoned mis-information through news and media and school systems since day 1- and that such a system taught prejudice and fear and through this segregation and reciprocated enmity. Whilst the whole time keeping everyone in the dark in more ways than one and therefore being *kept,* forever condemningly judgemental . . .

He was neither Pagan or Heathen as they were both Christian concepts. He founded True Enlightenment. Understanding, Nature, Love, God. He helped to communicate both telepathically, and physically, as well as on an invisible touch screen on occasion. Communicating True Mentality.

When he got high, everyone else got high. Everything was cool, the paranoia stopped. With the come down, you came down, and you all wanted to get him. It happened so many times that even you began to notice how you changed. You should stay feeling good the whole time as you take the positive experiences of getting high with you. Treat yourselves, and give him a fuckin break! Who doesn't want to feel good all the time?!

Every being in existence seeing, analysing, judging and spitting on ya every move and thought, when you cant control your thoughts and every waking moment was spent reeling back, whilst having to work. Try living with that paranoia he said.

But of course all this shit and then some, bombardment, which was the norm, as it became the norm the moment he made sense of it. Therefore he doesn't really seem that clever even though he was the one thinking it. Making sense of every thought possible and showing you complete clarity whilst keeping you away from the worst of if. He only lost track of 4 points along the Thought Path, (Metropolis) in the past 5 out of 6 years of solid thinking.

The only medication that truly works is there being someone there to understand what your saying and talking sense back. Anti psychotic medication, all the negative connotations that go with that term.

Better reflect on planet earth where no one sees it, or everyone in close proximity to you in the after-life will see your unresolved past and issues. Whilst the whole time on earth you took out your unresolved issues on everyone else as you looked down your nose at them. You will end up polluting the airways with shit. I wont be happy.

Every tone of voice, every thought that linked with every scenario as well as all of its links and all of those thoughts. We're all fundamentally the same as were all human, but were all different at the same time. That's the beauty of life, meeting new people. Everyone has a story to tell, everyone that has chosen to grow is unique.

Reflection. Resolving issues so that the toxic dead weight of burden dragging the scales below and polluting pure water, became annihilated. Through this, the water becomes pure, and the scales of True Loving Equality are above water, and we're all free to shine.

Things were so coincidental, that it seemed to him that fate, was fate.

Mentality, spirituality, whole heartedly in black hole. And how tortured a Soul is trapped in possessed atoms of Physical atoms of a Human automaton, and taken to Hell. How else would Anyone tell you. Body of just plain atoms, possessed by Evil One paedophile soul and spirituality, as far as that **is** possible. I'm sure he was very convincing. Ill answer for the evil one. Fuel my hatred towards it even more. Since time immemorial, almighty God, and Evil One paedophile. Who do you think is more powerful? That, or a 22 year old young man. The greatest trick the devil ever did was convincing you that it didn't exist. Well I'm telling you it does. And that's how it played its biggest part to date, to try and deter you from **Love**. that's how it left its mark. The greatest trick the devil ever did was convincing you that it didn't exist. It **Does.**

Paedos burn at the steak starting 21st of July, 2015. This is absolution for their sin. No one does anything again, **other**wise, they go to hell. An impenetrable capsule that hovers in pitch black, with most agonising, and tortuous pain switch that never eases, for the rest of eternity . . . You adhere to this date, you need me around til I'm 28. I'm 25 now.

The afterlife is a persons second chance. They need to burn **fully,** as they will become warriors that know absolute pain, as they fight the Good fight. You don't want those that have a baptism of fire supporting the evil one. They're genitals burn with them at the steak . . . Almighty God decides who goes to Hell.

You **Do** need my guidance over the next 2 and a half years for this to succeed. You Must **Stand.** Even those of you who support the evil one Must Rise and Fight the **Good** Fight. If Some part of you wants to go to **Heaven**, you do what is Right. No **Child** belongs in Hell.

SELECTION DAY

"So you all prepared?" Harmony asked her tutor with gusto, as she nibbled on her slice of melon in a cute manner.

"As ready as I'm ever gonna be . . ."

Filing the papers on his desk neatly into his briefcase, he bid farewell to one of his brightest pupils.

"Quietly confident as well Harmony. I believe people are beginning to see the light!"

Rising from his seat, he clicked smart shoes across the tiled floor and reached the door without hesitation,

"Good luck!" Harmony shouted to him in jubilation, "not that you'll need much of it I'm sure!"

Finishing her lunch, she wiped her mouth and the door clicked shut behind her tutor. looking to the white board, she read the instruction of the day which was to write a poem about how money and quality of life, was a product of physical manifestations of the universal sub-conscious, (as well as conscious), mind. Including issues not only of the Western world, but also that of everywhere else on planet earth. The masterpiece from Harmony had yet to be collected as she stayed at lunch to finish.

The course was a work in progress and as it progressed, it gradually led to complete knowledge and clarity developmental, as this particular philosophy led to answers.

She realised that her tutor had done his best to walk in his predecessors shoes after he was taken away.

As she articulated, she realised that knowledge was no longer secret, but freely obtainable, as people were beginning to see, and were no longer hindered by pigs on the wing. But of course, it was like an ultimatum that hung in the balance. These were tender times.

As the evening progressed,

"And the final count is -467 Enlightenment party, 469 National Guidance **Front**."

Toxic and mocking wolf whistles led by a melage of taunting. Half cheering and half booing was the accompaniment to such a dire farce and travesty.

"Looks like you lucked out boyo. Who would believe it! Losing by 2 votes, you couldn't ask for it to be any closer." The man laughed insidiously,

"So I take it then that free talk about topics such as **Free Energy Tesla** is illegal all over Britain now?" Hendrix said as his next and last lesson plan was snuffed out to a like that of a bright star.

What with oil companies that bleed mother nature dry—even pick at the scabs with fracking—and of course you not wanting it in place as they earn too much money off of mother nature's blood . . . Its all energy at the end if the day. **Mother Nature.**

And all the lesson plans, even those that have links to Enlightenment, are to be trodden out. They only knew about *links* because of True Enlightenment." But that's the way the system worked.

"Aye simple as that." the annoying man chortled, as he continued,

"Looks like you just broke the law. Don't worry though Hendrix, I wont report ya—This time."

Is That an Angel Hurtling toward Earth from the Heavens . . . ? Flock to my banner, there is an impenetrable wall there.

That night as Marcy cleaned in the utter silence which was keystone college, and just about to leave for the night, She looked to the poem that once twisted a knife in her mentality.

'Hendrix cares for no body, but EveryOne—'

Universal Chaos. I'm the one that made sense of it all and told you.

If the Government ever initiate the purge (all crime is legal for 5 hours, you don't want that), head to your local drug dealer . . . wow—where have you been all my life! They would do it to reduce human population, and then they come in with brute military; order out of ultimate force on your reeling and giddy senses. You don't want warring on the streets, as martial law is a Big NO NO. We need to liberate Syria from its murderous and tyrannical government, before Korea make a launch system big enough. Peace Keeping Boots, on the ground

With power comes great responsibility.

2 years of good life for everyone, then the true witch and wizard hunts begin. You put up with them so long, now just 2 more years. Mental issues need to be resolved on planet Earth with no thought of harbouring any of that shit to the afterlife.

Life Must Blossom. Take my word for it. Be nice to everyone you meet, regardless, even though some wounds will never heal, those that you don't get along with, just ignore.

If anyone writes anything contrary to this, they're supporting evil one paedophile. He also knows everything we know.

If you still have a problem, the book obviously hasn't sunk in yet. Perhaps you should read it again at some point.

Why like, we're always out to get someone.

They'll spend a pretzel on it, then they'll look like the saviours. Quickly before all land turns to mush, rise. Kick out those free masons who like to grow your food in a vat. Consumed with consuming your consumerism. Embrace Life. You've been told. Its just become second nature to you to be told how to live your life,

If you feel a dull ache in your shoulder, that's your wings budding. Shoot out your wing by shooting your finger from base point, mid point and high point of the ache, to the side of your body. Remember this because if you feel that ache and you don't do anything about it, you might end up having a heart attack. You earn your wings. No matter what iv done, 1 man isn't important enough. Except Jesus. And me, for the time being.

You need a good foundation, so don't play a little game. Unless it's a friendly one that doesn't harm in any way. This is a tender couple of years. Idiom sins critic. If you ever receive any dodgy texts from my phone, it aint me. I aint like that.

Your every day waking life will sort and become more of a fuller reality to a lot of our older generation, even our generation. Put it into practice. The 2 books. The one in the middle making plain sense of they're dispute. Metaphor (the Globe). **Rise.** we need that Yellow Pearl. We serve God. Hell is the worst. None of us want Hell. You will live in constant Fear, and you think its bad now, No? I have told you the worst, through this book. It will be a billion times worse. And it will continue to just get worse and worse. It is Hell. Nothing glamorous, it's the worst!! How else do you think the Evil One paedophile would leave its mark and try and confuse. What irony as I'm the one setting you free. Its not in it for the fame. It's the worst. On a separate note, I'm in it, for the rest of you. (the devil put all its eggs in one basket with me)

With Free Energy Tesla in place, the land wouldn't melt into the sea, as it is a clean infinite form of energy. Even the particles that make up an atom have a magnetic field that has been harnessed to create infinite clean energy. It has already been invented, but of course the oil companies don't want that in place as they make far too much money from bleeding and picking the scabs of Mother Nature dry.

A senate. A Voice of the People. Suggestion boxes. All that money that would be taken from those 5 to 25 banker families, and spent on the People. As they take from us a lot including Soul a lot of the time. But have Faith, and Serve God. He knows everything and wants what's best for us. We need that Yellow Pearl! Aye, life's hard. Freedom! Rise!

If the brave men and women of our armed forces are going to die, they should die Liberating, not warring. We all share suffering in common. I hate to see suffering.

Arbiter. Did you have to queue up for your poetic licence? that's the reason why drugs are illegal. The GOVERNment don't want you opening your Mind. Plus they don't want to see you having a good time. Kick them **Out!** you think this is bad? There will be complete lock down. You wont even be allowed to drink your drug. Partying, what's that? That's no longer allowed, except for the hierarchy. That's what it will be if you don't RISE! And that will only be the start of how bad things would get if you don't Rise.

Wouldn't you rather a persons free choice to do, what the fuck they want to do, unhindered? Whilst sticking to the laws of self control and equality.

This isn't just some poetic way of putting life. This is Life. Do something about it. Stand and be counted for the right to Peace! Of course the Western World are the biggest terrorists of them all. They were responsible for the twin towers you know. They just hide behind a vale that I have lifted for you all. Let the fifteens off with a severe kick in. if they do it again, they go to Hell. Our 'fascist' hierarchy had nothing to do in life except control, and ultimately own us. And you would be astounded to see how they fuck with us. And they'll be in the last city on planet Earth, all the white haired bald fuckers who think they have the ultimate right to life as they went about theirs, raping and pillaging. However, the land wont be swallowed by the sea, with **Free Energy Tesla** in place. It has already been patented and works! Oh yeah, everything seems so obvious now! Whos the man telling you . . .

Life is not a joke, it's a very precious thing.

Paedos that do pass on, if they don't go to Hell, you can live in hope. But I'm telling ya, you serve God. You get to keep your genitalia, let that be your one saving grace as the battle between good and evil, you fight for God. You shouldn't have done it. You do it again, you go to Hell. You serve God! We need warriors that know absolute pain, fighting for God. You wouldn't believe how rife it wis. There will be a lot of them.

All issues have been resolved by your older brother Lee. But of course not all issues have been resolved as you still have your unresolved past to deal with and sort out.

If you hear a voice across the airways after the 21st of January 2016, tell it to shut the fuck up and show some respect, for it will not be me, your liberator. It will just be some jumped up little prick trying to confuse you. And if you ever hear the antichrist whispering in your ear dark temptations or fear mongering, tell that evil cunt to sling his hook.

No matter how clever or melodious messages across the airways sound, ignore it, there is nothing left to say. However, you must stick with Jesus. You fight the good fight.

Tell Russia to back the fuck off, or if possible, join with us as we liberate these little countries from they're murderous and tyrannical hierarchies. Remember, the western world is just as bad, they just smother it up. Most of our hierarchy are paedos anyway. Your being owned by paedophiles. There will be Hell if you do not RISE!!

I burn on the 21st of January 2016.

I never said that 'I', was Lee in the book.

All drugs should be legalised except for crack cocaine, heroin, crystal meth, peyote and mescaline, PCP, acid and mushrooms.

Trying to defuse this ticking time bomb. Peaceful protests or there will be martial law. We don't stop til they're **Booted Out!** Why should we pay the ultimate price and answer for our warmongering, terrorist, occultist, **Paedophilic hierarchy**!

Oh cos life got too hard so he decided to do himself in? I don't think so. The scars on my arms and wrists are because of Psychiatry. RESPECT! We're like mules to the pharmaceutical companies who give us Side Effect medication, then extra medication for the side effects. We're like guini pigs to them. The only medication that truly works is someone being there to understand what your saying and talk sense back.

There all in it for the money and power. Not you, your loved ones or me. As they, (as well as the system) go about earning billions and trillions, keeping us all in the dark in more ways than one, laughing all the way to the **banks**. Yes I do also know about the NHS. I hate medication.

I already found fibre optic cable in the headboard of my bed.

God was pierced in his right heel by pure evil as he reached for the suspended in animation Yellow Pearl. A barrier has been created but we must all pull together and get Rid of evil completely and expel it. Just a metaphor. Oh yeah, cos I ended it on that does that cause you to forget the other true and real points. Impatience is a vice.

A lot to take in. Read it again at some point.

There are biomasses growing in pipe lines and shower walls. You ever wonder what that wet sucking sound is in your maintenance? In some strange way, it could be nano technology. I know these things are dangerous. I've probably got the biggest one in my flat at the moment. This thing moves with no food. There are some things that I don't know. But this modern day and new age of Spirituality, all is Real.

Ignorance will be Hell. 3rd world debt should be nullified, as there is enough money on planet Earth, for everyone to have a life of luxury free from a murderous, tyrannical paedophilic hierarchy breathing down your neck trying to take COMPLETE CONTROL!

Some people don't know how good we have it. You don't think so? Then I'm telling you there will be Hell if you don't Rise. Compared to Loving Totality if you all rise and kick out that paedophilic business of crooks that own us all. (I mean how hard is it?)

We have been kept in the dark in more ways than one and it has been preconditioned into us that the life we lead is acceptable. Whilst Children still Die of Starvation.

There will be Hell if you don't rise. No one wants Hell. Just imagine the worst day of your life, make it a Billion times worse, whilst getting worse and worse and worse, all the way up to infinity. (For the rest of eternity!)

Now do you hear the urgency in my voice. Whilst of course, evil one paedophile raping for eternity. This is what will take place if you don't rise, and keep me around til I'm 28.

Now do you see the urgency in my pledge to you. You must Rise! We DON'T STOP Peacefully demonstrating in a clever way until they are booted out. Say as an educated population that we don't need to be governed or ruled by **SLUGS**.

If I'm not around to wrangle it back round from the chaos that would be you looking down your nose at everyone (reciprocated enmity), remember, the looking has stopped. And you honestly think I haven't noticed. I don't brag, but I'm the brightest shining Level 3 around. You earn your wings. The highest level a human will ever be is a level three. There is no greater honour than getting your wings.

Muslims, learn not to hate the western world in this new age, we will provide you with a life of luxury, as we topple our warmongering hierarchy's who spoil it for your common man.

The evil one paedophile will continue to rape unless you leave me around til I'm 28. My Death is done **MY WAY.** If you want rid of me before I'm 28, **Other**Wise you would be supporting evil one paedophile. You would be supporting ultimate paedophilia.

If one person puts it out of kilter, and I wasn't around, who would be there to wrangle it back round from the chaos that would be everyone looking down they're nose at each other. Look how it sleuths into the room with its many guises and inSidiosity and fucks with you. Kick it away. You defend the light.

You need to learn over the next 2 and a quarter years. You will become a fuller being when you look inside yourself, as when you search, you will find answers. You wont be shot off down some schizoid path, there is solidity to it.

When you look inside yourself, reflect on planet Earth and learn, not only from your mistakes, so you don't make any more big ones. When you look and learn, leave each other alone for the next 2 years, some wounds will never heal, those people you don't get along with, you just ignore. With greater understanding, when you look inside yourself, some things you will rise above. Impatience is a vice.

2 years of good life for everyone. How strong you will be and how bright you will all shine

When you Embrace God!

Lots of people talkin, few of them know, soul of a woman was created below (LZ). Even if soul of a woman was created below, who doesn't want the BEST afterlife for eternity?! Sell your Souls to God!

Realisation, with no funky shit.

All issues have been resolved by you older brother Lee, me. But of course, not all issues have been resolved, as you still all have to look inside yourselves. But of course, all issues have been resolved.

When you search, you will find answers. No one sees your reflection. Believe that. If you want your lives to be a Million times better all the way up to Infinity, you must RISE!!! HUMANITY!

Plain English. Don't let anyone bastardise the English Language. Plain English. You earn your wings. The only level anyone will ever Reach on planet Earth is a level 3, There is no greater honour than getting your wings. There should be nothing in place which dictates that Light should be offered by dark. Rise Now or your lives will take a severe nose dive.

Don't hate me for it. It will be a walk in the park for you in comparison. The last trick the devil ever pulled was convincing you that it was God that was responsible for the ultimate pain you felt. It's the devil that makes you suffer, not God. Ignorance will be Hell. If you don't Rise, there will be Hell for Eternity. No one wants Hell.

The shit talk **Stops.** Look inside yourself, you will become fuller, and that's when the true connections begin. A New Age of **Spirituality.**

Enjoy **Life**, with your new found **Enlightenment**

Lightning Source UK Ltd.
Milton Keynes UK
UKOW03f0453260314

228826UK00002B/107/P